I0682482

Seeds Of Lust
Sexy Stories Collection

VOLUME 31

16 EROTIC SHORT STORIES

BLAINE TELLER

Publisher's Note: This is a work of fiction.
Names, characters, places, and incidents are a
product of the author's imagination. Locales and
public names are sometimes used for
atmospheric purposes. Any resemblance to
actual people, living or dead, or to businesses,
companies, events, institutions, or locales is
completely coincidental.

Seeds Of Lust/ Blaine Teller. -- 1st ed.
Xplicit Press, an imprint of TLM Media LLC

ISBN-13: 978-1-62327-562-4
ISBN-10: 1-62327-562-8
eISBN: 978-1-62327-613-3

Printed in the United States of America

CONTENTS

1   Foxy Lady   1

2   Master Baking   17

3   The Seed Of Courage   29

4   Fully Mooned   43

5   Getting Slaid   61

6   Girly   71

7   Girlier: Girly Part 2   81

8   Need   91

9   Demon Seed   107

10 Safari   119

CONTENTS

11 Gridiron Girls   141

12 Blue Screen Of Desire   155

13 A Woman's Touch   165

14 Siren's Song   175

15 Visitor   189

16 Witch's Ball   199

1 FOXY LADY

My eyes half-heartedly observed the television, no part of me interested in what I was seeing. This cheesy, interchangeable romance flick had gone from predictable to insipid within minutes. And yet, I still endured. Not for my own sake, but for the blonde on my right. It was her turn to pick a movie and I didn't flinch when I saw her selection. Fair is fair, after all. Still, I probably could have quoted this entire film word-for-word without even having seen it. After a certain point it ceased to even be cheesy dialogue, and instead just sounded like an endless barrage of slogans lifted directly from "romantic" greeting cards.

After an hour of fluff and nonsense, there came a sex scene. I casually averted my gaze from the screen. There was nothing interesting about watching actors slap their groins together. I instead let my eyes drift over to my girlfriend. Her long, toned legs disappeared into a short, denim skirt. Her upper body was clad in only a camouflage tank top that left her arms, neck, and much of her cleavage exposed. She had a fairly deep tan on most of her exposed skin, but her tank top had shifted a bit and I could just barely see some of her tan lines in the dull light given off by the TV. Her shoulder-length, ash blonde hair was immaculately straightened. She had a colored accent stripe in the front; light metallic blue that steadily darkened along the way to a black tip. The color somewhere in the middle of the stripe matched her eyes.

She was attractive, or at least that's what people said. I really have no frame of reference for human attractiveness. I did like her, but much more for her personality than her looks. That, and when people saw me with her, they could feel confident in my normalcy. People have said that I am attractive as well, but I don't see it in myself either. Skinny, black hair, brown eyes, just the beginnings of a farmer's tan. I took comfort in the idea of feeling plain, but I couldn't imagine myself as hot. Maybe it had something to do with my face-blindness. I've never had an easy time telling people apart by their faces - they all sort of look the same to me. I have to tell people apart by their voices, their clothes, or their hair. Fortunately, Amber always made it easy to recognize her hair.

A playful smirk crossed my lips in the

darkness. Next week, when it was my turn to pick a movie, I should make her sit through an animal mating documentary. Then I could be the one feeling tingly while she sat there, bored! Just as the silly revenge fantasy crossed my mind, I felt a hand on my crotch. Amber legitimately caught me by surprise; I nearly jumped out of my skin. She had crawled closer while I wasn't paying attention. One arm over the back of the couch, the other feeling me up, she was sitting nearly close enough for our faces to touch.

"Evan, this movie sucks. Let's go make our own sex scene."

I was stunned. Though pleased at her criticism of the film, the rest of what I heard made me uncomfortable. "I don't know about that. I'm not sure I'm ready to go there."

"Oh come on, you're a guy! Guys always think about sex."

"Thinking doesn't mean we necessarily feel like going through with it. And besides, not all guys have sex on the brain all the time."

"Human sex, you mean. You think about it just as much, but with animals."

My eyes went wide. "I do not! How did you find out about that? Whoever told you that was lying."

Amber laughed. "No one told me, I just know. I also know you don't think I'm pretty, and that you're dating me so nobody will think you're weird."

"What? How?" I lowered my head. "I'm

sorry Amber, I didn't think you'd find out. That's wrong and I apologize."

"I don't know what you're so worried about. I don't think anyone looks at a single guy and automatically assumes he's into animals."

"How do you even know this?"

"You wouldn't believe me if I told you."

"Just tell me."

"I can read minds, Evan."

"Liar."

"No, really."

"Okay, then what am I..."

"Seven. A big yellow seven with orange polka dots."

"That's insane! How can you even do that?"

She shrugged. "It's just a gift I have. I don't know how I got to be this way, I just always have been. There's something else I can do, too. It's pretty amazing, I think you'll enjoy it."

"What is it?"

"I'm not going to tell you, I think it would be better if I showed you instead." She stood and offered me a hand. "Come on, let's go to bed and I'll show you there. Sleeping with me won't be as awkward as you think, I promise."

I accepted her help standing, though I didn't really need it. She walked down the hall, and I nervously followed. "So, are we through, or...?"

"That's up to you. I like you, and I know you like me. I'm not going to dump you for not wanting to have sex, though I'd ask you to reserve judgment until you see my other trick."

She led me to her bedroom and crawled atop a big fluffy comforter. Lying on her side, she patted the spot next to her. I hesitated for a moment, then got into bed with her. She got onto her hands and knees, then made her way towards me. The predatory gleam in her eyes had me a little worried. As she came closer, I reflexively edged back until I had scrunched myself up against the headboard. She kept coming until her nose was right next to mine.

"What? Are you afraid to kiss me now?"

"Oh! I didn't know that's what you were..."

She shut me up with a kiss, then giggled and sat up on her knees. "Silly boy."

"So, what's this trick of yours that's going to make me function like a normal person?"

Amber shook her head. "Oh no, Evan sweetie. My powers can't make you more attracted to the human body."

"Powers?"

"Yes, powers. I can, however, take a form more compatible with your sexual orientation."

"Are you saying what I think you're saying?"

"See, this is why I wasn't going to say anything. It would be so much easier if I just did it. Here, watch."

Her skin began to glow brightly. As the light blurred her figure, I could see nothing but a white silhouette. That silhouette changed shape right before my very eyes, shifting and shrinking until it had taken the shape of a vixen. The light faded, and a blue eyed fox sat within a small pile of Amber's clothes. She crawled out of the top, skirt, bra, and panties to make her way over to me. Most of her body was covered in beautiful orange fur, but her cheeks, neck, belly, and tail tip were pure white. Her ears, paws, and part of her legs were black. It made her look like she had little stockings on.

To my astonishment, this animal spoke in Amber's voice. “How do I look?”

“You look gorgeous!”

“Thank you. I couldn't match your favorite fantasy exactly. I would do the gold eyes for you if I could, but that's the one thing I can't change.”

“Oh, blue eyes look even better. The way they contrast your orange fur just makes you look even more amazing.”

I told myself there was no way this could actually happen. Mind reading and shapeshifting aren't scientifically possible ... the past few minutes couldn't have happened. I must have fallen asleep during the movie and this was just a perfect dream. Even as I tried to get my head on straight, the sexy little fox walked along my body until her muzzle met my lips. I could feel her whiskers on my face, shattering any illusion that this wasn’t really happening. I opened my mouth and accepted her tongue. Then, I gave her mine. I closed my eyes and ran my fingers through her warm fur.

Much too soon, Amber broke away from

the tender smooch. "So, do you think you could comfortably shag me like this?"

"I think so. I mean yes, I definitely could. But, is that okay? I don't want to hurt your feelings or anything."

She laughed. Seeing all of her sharp teeth was a little unnerving. "Evan, I'm me. As a shapeshifter, I don't get attached to any one form. Changing species for me is like changing clothes for someone else. Telling me that my human form is a boner deterrent isn't any more offensive than telling anyone else you don't like their shirt." One of her little paws pressed on my crotch. "I want to have sex with my boyfriend. Turning into an animal is barely an effort for me. If it makes things more comfortable for you, then I don't mind a bit."

"Thank you. I've always been so afraid to live out my fantasies. I'm scared I'll hurt an animal if I try to and that bothers me. But if you can do this..."

"I'm the best of both worlds, I can satisfy you in bed and still preserve your social acceptability. But speaking of satisfying in bed, let's save this sappy stuff for later. I'm really horny right now."

Amber hopped off of my chest and turned her back to me. Standing near the middle of the bed, she lifted her tail to give me an uninhibited view of her fox holes. The sight was so beautiful, I thought my heart would stop. I slid off of the bed and wasted no time in stripping out of my clothes. I crawled up onto the comforter, sitting on my knees. The vixen stuck her head between my legs and began to eagerly lick my balls and semi-erect cock. I groaned and stroked her fur while she worked me over. That hot, strong tongue of hers had me rock hard in no time.

Once I was properly stiff, she closed her muzzle around my length. I was nervous because of her teeth, but she knew what she was doing. The little fox held the whole thing in her muzzle and suckled, stroking the underside of it with her tongue. I could just barely feel the points of her teeth on my meat, if she moved her mouth she would scrape me. But she kept her muzzle still, and only held me with as much pressure as she needed to suck me. The feel of her hot mouth wrapped around my sensitive cock was incredible, I knew I didn't have much hope of holding back like this.

Amber looked up at me the entire time, staring into my plain brown eyes with her sparkly blue ones. She'd said her eyes were the same in any form, but I hadn't noticed how lovely they were before. They glimmered like amethysts – it's true, no matter how cheesy it sounds. My hand crept down her body, across her back and to her bottom. She was making me feel good, and I wanted to give back. My fingers found her tiny fox pussy, and I slowly stroked her outer lips. She moaned for me, sending vibrations through my cock. I stroked harder, and she moaned louder.

I was edging closer by the second. I could feel myself ready to pop. When she brought one of her warm little paws up to play with my nuts, I lost it. My head jerked back and a groan of bliss escaped my lips. At the same instant, she released my tool from her lovely muzzle's grasp. Her tongue flicked out to exquisitely caress my cock head with each shot of cum I gave. Her timing was flawless. That paw of hers kept working my balls, too. She was milking me for every drop I could give. The licking continued even after I'd finished cumming, and the contact on my over-sensitive post-orgasmic organ made me squirm.

When the fox was done teasing me, she provided a final lick from the back of my balls to the tip of my dick and then stepped away. She rolled onto her back, her hind legs open wide in an inviting posture. I gave the vixen an appreciative kiss on the muzzle, then got down between her thighs. It was my turn to provide oral favors, and I intended to give as good as I got. I slid my tongue across her slit experimentally, and found her flavor enjoyable. I couldn't tell if it was part of her shapeshifting ability or if foxes are just naturally flavorful, but she was quite sweet.

After a few teasing licks along her outer folds, I pressed my tongue between her lips and wiggled it against her inner labia. I'd never done this before, but I listened to her vocalizations for clues on what I was doing right. It was strange to hear a fox making human sex sounds, but if she could talk like a woman then what's to say she can't moan like a woman? I pushed the distraction from my head and focused on the task at hand.

I ran a hand up and down her soft, white, furry tummy. I could feel her stiff nipples beneath the fur, and made sure to stroke them while I rubbed her belly. I brought my other hand down to open her up with two fingers. With her lips spread, I was able to push my tongue up into her. Her tightness provided some resistance against my thick tongue, but she was certainly appreciative when I got it in there. Once comfortably inside, I moved my fingers away from her puffy folds. Instead, I lightly tickled her puckered anus. She clenched when I touched it. I made her squirm by lightly tracing my fingertip around the rim.

My fleshy, pink oral organ wriggled inside the vixen's yummy snatch, tasting every surface I could reach inside her. She let out a short, sharp cry when my tongue grazed a rough patch inside her. I smiled. That had definitely sounded more fox-like. I worked my tongue against that spot specifically, pushing hard against the rough patch and sliding back and forth.

Amber bucked her hips, her breath came in short pants. "Right there, that's the spot! Now ride it until I cum!"

I did as the vixen asked, grinding my tongue hard against her g-spot. My hands kept teasing her nipples and ass as I licked. I wanted to give her as much pleasure as possible. Her hips bucked faster, and her soft moans slowly rose in volume. At last, she arched her back and screamed. A splash of slippery, cloudy girl cum exploded in my face. I slowly withdrew my tongue from her satisfied foxhole and licked some of the clear honey from her outer lips. The taste was even more exquisite than her pre-climax pussy juice.

After making her squirm for a little while, I sat up on my knees. My cock was fully hard again, throbbing with need. I grabbed her legs and pulled her closer, then rubbed my meat against her slippery little slit. It was only now, seeing my dick so close to her entrance, that I realized how significant the size difference really was. I suddenly became a little uncertain.

"Am I going to fit into you?"

"Of course!"

"But you're so small."

"If you were doing this with a real vixen, you'd need to use some artificial lubricant and go slowly. You're actually about average fox length, but your shaft is thicker than a fox's shaft would be. It's not as thick as a fox's knot, though, so I doubt a real fox would have too much trouble taking it."

"Are foxes really that big?" I realized immediately after saying this that it was kind of a silly question. I, myself, came in a little below average for my own species, so it's not like we were talking about anything truly large.

"Canids in general tend to be well-equipped for their size. I'm not a real fox, though. As a shapeshifter I can alter my insides however I like. I could have sex with a horse while in this form, if I wanted to. I don't particularly want to, but I have the option. I'm wet enough for you to slide in, no artificial slippery needed. You can take me good and hard, if you want. Don't worry, I'll tell you if you hurt me."

I nudged the tip of my cock between her folds and shivered. This was usually when I'd wake up from a dirty dream. With another soft push, I buried my dick head in her tight embrace. We both moaned in unison, our vocalizations making a beautiful harmony. I held my place there for a moment, just savoring the feel of her wrapped around me. My hips moved forward a little at a time, inching my way into her burning-hot muffin. I watched my pulsing rod disappear into her impossibly tight folds, until finally I bottomed out in her. I could feel my balls resting on the base of her tail.

It took a feat of willpower to pull out of such a lovely place, even though I knew I was going right back in. I slid back until I was halfway inside, then pushed all the way in again. I took Amber in smooth, slow strokes. My hands slid up and down her body, caressing her soft fur. Her pussy was unbelievable, nothing I'd ever done to myself could hope to compare. Every time she clenched, I felt it in my entire body. I luxuriated in her sensuous form, taking my time to savor every second of mating with her.

I wanted the incredible feeling to last forever, but I could already feel a climax approaching. Her foxy body was just too tight, too hot, too incredible for me to stand a chance of holding it in. I gave her a few more steady, deep strokes. And then, I pulled out of her completely. My swollen glans slid free of her slippery pink vice, and not a second too soon. Any longer and I would have lost it. My cock twitched and throbbed madly, almost as if it were trying to escape my crotch.

Amber didn't ask what I was doing. She didn't even wait for me to ask her to roll over. My shapeshifting vixen lover knew exactly what I was thinking, and rolled to her feet. Facing away, tail held high, she waited until I was ready to get back inside her. I took a minute or so to calm down, I didn't want to pop right away. My engorged shaft relaxed into a much healthier looking, normal erection. Satisfied that I could spend a little longer inside her without finishing now, I got behind the fox and lined myself up.

Once the head of my cock was inside her again, I grabbed her hips with both hands. With a single push, I buried my entire length in her foxy pussy. My hips rolled as fast as I could possibly move them, pounding my cock in and out of her rapidly. I did my best impression of a male fox, humping Amber like I was trying to break her. The way she was moaning made it pretty clear that she favored fast, rough sex. Her pleasured cries only encouraged me further.

I gritted my teeth and tried to make it last. Her tightness and my speed wouldn't allow me to hold back very long with any amount of effort, and I was already close to begin with. Suddenly, she came with a scream and a tight clench. The feel of her squeezing around my meat, and the hot wash of fluids on my crotch catapulted me over the edge. I shoved all the way into her and cried out. My dick pulsed hard inside her, firing a thick rope of seed with every throb. I ground my hips against her backside, milking myself into her.

It took a few minutes for me to summon the willpower to pull out of Amber. The feel of her hot inner walls grinding against my cock head the whole way out made me squirm. Finally, my dick popped free of her little sex oven. She turned around and started licking my tender meat, cleaning the mess of mixed fluids. Once she'd cleaned my dick, she moved on to lap her own juices out of my pubic hair and off of my balls. Satisfied that she'd given me a thorough tongue-bath, she curled up to lick the fluids from her pussy.

"Must be nice to be that flexible."

Amber giggled. "Oh, it is. Once you've gotten off on your own tongue, you just can't do it by hand anymore."

She went back to slurping her slit, though in a mostly non-sexual way. Once she wasn't oozing semen anymore, she stood and stretched. Then, she nuzzled me and licked my lips. I kissed her again, deep and with tongue. I could taste a little of my own cum in her mouth, but I didn't particularly mind.

After the kiss, Amber stepped back and began to glow again. Her body re-shaped itself and took human form once more. I had never seen her naked before. Her body still didn't wow me in this shape, but I couldn't unsee how pretty her eyes were, regardless of what the rest of her looked like. My eyes were drawn to her tan lines, though, but only because of the contrast. They formed the shape of a bikini on her skin. I can't remember seeing her in a bikini in the whole time I've known her.

"They are."

"What?"

"You were wondering if my tan lines are a part of my shapeshifting. They are. I can have them year round if I like. I can change anything about myself whenever I want. I don't even actually dye my hair."

"That seems like a really useful power to have."

Amber smiled. "Quite so, it got me laid tonight."

Now it was my turn to smile. "Thank you, Amber. I didn't think I'd ever get the chance to actually do something like this. That was incredible!"

"You were pretty good yourself. I haven't been fucked that good in a long time."

Amber peeled back the comforter and sheets, then crawled in and got cozy. I slid under the comforter as well and put my arm around her. She pressed her body close to mine. I stroked her back affectionately. As I dozed off, I couldn't help but wonder if she could see my dreams as well. I was asleep before I could explore the idea much further.

2 MASTER BAKING

Heather Dawson, world renowned baker, had delighted people for years with her special-recipe baked goods. Everything she made had an extra zing to it, a burst of sweet flavor that put it far ahead of her competition. People flew in from continents away just to eat her cakes and cookies. Throughout Heather's long and distinguished career, she had consistently refused to sell any of her recipes for mass production. She had also never revealed the secret ingredient that made her baked goods so special, nor had anyone managed to figure it out.

Lately, the flavor she was famous for had begun to weaken. Many people speculated that the tough economy had impacted her ability to purchase the quality ingredients she uses. The more pessimistic instead claimed she had given up. In truth, she was just getting old. Which was why she'd taken on an apprentice, someone she could train as her replacement.

Kimberly Hong was a brash and irritable young woman, quick to anger and difficult to placate. She'd been offered her apprenticeship fresh out of culinary school, and had leapt at the chance to work with the legendary Heather Dawson. The past two weeks had been stressful for them both, however.

Heather had kept her secret ingredient hidden from Kimberly for the first two weeks of the apprenticeship, instead giving her a training course in baking. Kimberly continually insisted that she was learning nothing she didn't already know and her attitude wore Heather thin. The crash course in basic business management had gone more smoothly, but Kimberly had continued to prod about the secret ingredient despite Heather's insistence that she would know when she's ready.

Heather stood in the kitchen, waiting for her apprentice to arrive. Her auburn hair was streaked with gray, and tied back in a bun. Crow's feet framed her tired, green eyes. Her naturally large breasts had come to sag significantly, an inevitable part of the aging process.

Kimberly turned her key in the lock and entered the kitchen behind Dawson's

Bakery. The Chinese-American girl wore a dark scowl on her face, broadcasting her hatred of early morning. Her warm, brown eyes expressed more emotion than her mouth seemed capable of most of the time. Though naturally black, her hair had been bleached and then dyed bright crimson. Her body was slim, taut, and perky everywhere. The mere sight of her filled Heather with a mixture of envy and lust.

"Good morning Kimberly."

"Morning. What are we learning today?"

"What you've been so eager to learn for a good while now. Today, you learn what the secret ingredient is, where it comes from, and how to harvest it. Though, I suspect you already know that last one."

"It better not be something obvious."

"It isn't. When I tell you, you may not even believe me."

"So spit it out already."

"Always so impatient, Kimberly. Baking is mostly waiting, so why can't you treat life more like baked goods?"

"I can only stomach so much waiting, and I use it all up on baking."

"Fair enough. Before I tell you what my secret is, I should let you know that what happens today can make or break your chances of succeeding me."

"What? You're saying you might drop me after telling me your secret? Why?"

"A practical reason, I assure you. The secret ingredient is a very personal thing; no two bakers can make it exactly the same. I only took on an apprentice in the first place because I can't make it the way I used to. If your version of the secret ingredient isn't flavorful enough, there's no point in you taking over for me."

"Then why not tell me this up front? Why wait so damn long?"

"Because the secret would shock you. I needed you to have a lot of time invested in this so it will be harder for you to just leave if you don't like what I tell you."

"Stop dancing around the issue! What is it that made you so famous?"

"Cum. I masturbate into containers and add it to all of my recipes."

"No way! You're shitting me."

"I shit you not Kimberly. The reason my baked goods taste so amazing is because I came in all of them."

Kimberly laughed. "That's so twisted, I love it!"

"Good, I was worried you'd be disgusted."

"Disgusted? I'm getting a chance to make people from all over the world eat my cum! I want this job more than ever! Some of those interview questions make a lot more sense now, too. I've been wondering why being a squirter and having multiple orgasms have anything to do with apprenticing at a bakery."

"Good, good. Now, let's get nude."

Kimberly hiked a brow. "Why?"

"So I can taste you. I have to see if your flavor is suitable."

"Whoa, I thought you were going to give me a little plastic cup or something!"

"I find it's best when it's straight from the

source."

"Okay, I'll cum for you. Right in your face. But I want to lick you too, and I get to be on top. I'm always on top."

"I have no problem with any of that."

Both women removed their clothes, exposing their nude bodies to each other entirely. Heather was the first to get fully nude, and climbed up onto the counter. She lied on her back, getting as comfortable as she could on the hard surface.

"We're going to do it on the counter?"

"Why not? It'll wipe off easily."

"It just seems a little unsanitary."

"There's a reason I asked you not to put dough on this part of the counter."

"So that's like a designated sex spot?"

"Mostly masturbation and naps before you came along."

Kimberly finished undressing and climbed up onto the counter with Heather. She positioned herself above her mentor, facing the opposite way so that each woman had easy access to the other's pussy. Heather took the first few licks, wedging her tongue between Kimberly's folds and showing off her skill.

Kim shuddered and let out a long moan. "You're good at this."

"I went to an all girls school. I learned more about cunnilingus than any other subject."

Kimberly sampled Heather's pussy, rapidly flicking her tongue back and forth as she licked. She'd never tongued another girl before, and only had what she'd seen online to go on. The older woman's moans told her she was doing something right, though. Her hands slid along Heather's thighs while she enthusiastically slurped.

Heather buried her tongue in Kim's juicy twat again, and began using her talents to their fullest extent. Kimberly bucked her hips and shuddered. She'd never had such a talented, experienced lover between her legs. She desperately tried to give as good as she got, eventually adding her fingers to provide more sensations. Kim just couldn't keep up with Heather's tongue, for no lack of trying.

Kimberly humped her mentor's face, powerless to stop herself. Her shaved twat oozed slippery sweetness, and Heather didn't allow a drop to get away. The apprentice's nectar was sweet and strong, the taste driving Heather to work even harder at pleasuring her. Kim fought to keep up her efforts, frantically stroking Heather's g-spot and licking her clit. Her concentration was weakening, though.

When Heather slapped Kim's ass, the apprentice lost it. Kimberly arched, threw her head back, and screamed. Her tight, pink pussy shot many high-velocity streams of viscous girl-goo all over Heather's face. The master baker caught Kimberly's emissions in her mouth when she could, but happily accepted several blasts to the face as well. Her apprentice had a very intense, sweet flavor that she couldn't get enough of.

Kim took a few seconds to recover from her intense orgasm, then set about returning the favor. Her hand moved like a blur, pumping her fingers in and out of Heather's muff at lightning speed. The older woman bucked her hips and screamed, easily blown away by her apprentice's youthful enthusiasm. Within minutes, Heather's sweet fluids began to splash out of her glistening honeypot. Her squirting was less directed than Kimberly's, and instead came in numerous wet waves that coated Kim's face and neck. Quite a bit also splashed onto the counter and formed little puddles. Kimberly found the flavor quite familiar, and any doubt that Heather told the truth was effectively banished.

The two women rested in that position for a few minutes, licking and caressing each other affectionately. Kimberly bit Heather on the thigh, just hard enough to make her gasp. Heather gave Kim a firm swat on the ass, leaving a red hand print. Kim spun around and kissed Heather on the lips, an act the older woman happily accepted and reciprocated. They held the kiss for well over a minute, grinding and caressing while their tongues wrestled.

Kimberly broke the kiss. "So, do I pass the test?"

"With flying colors! You taste even better than I used to, you're going to do amazing things with this bakery. Now, if you're ready, we'll need to harvest a bunch of your cum so we can use it for today's baking."

Kimberly slid off of Heather, sitting on her knees atop the counter. "Sure, I'm ready. What do I need to do?"

Heather got up on her knees as well and

grabbed one of several large glass jars. "Squat over this, I'll finger you until it's full."

Kim did as she was told, positioning herself over the jar as comfortably as possible. Heather got behind her and kissed her neck. The older woman's left hand slid down to enthusiastically finger Kimberly from behind, while Heather's right hand made its way down Kim's front to work her clit. The master baker moved swiftly, with the intent to make Kimberly cum as fast and hard as possible.

The apprentice leaned back slightly, feeling Heather's tits squish against her back. Her own hands kneaded at her small, perky breasts to further enhance the amazing sensations wracking her body. She relaxed and let Heather go to town on her, without so much as a thought of holding back.

After a few minutes of frantic finger-banging, Kimberly shuddered her way through a screaming orgasm. Her slippery lady honey exploded into the jar below, and her position ensured none of it went to waste. Heather's hands didn't stop or even slow their expert ministrations, and Kim soon had another productive orgasm. Each successive climax made Kimberly more sensitive to Heather's attentions, and helped her reach the next peak that much faster.

Kimberly ejaculated again and again, orgasm after orgasm after orgasm. When a jar got full, she was given a few brief seconds of rest while Heather switched it out for an empty one. She watched as the collection of filled jars slowly grew, each brimming with her cloudy fem-spunk. After a while, Heather's fingers got tired so they switched tasks. Kim fingered herself in the same manner Heather had done, while Heather played with those perky titties.

The apprentice could barely breathe, her orgasms were coming so close together. Her body wasn't used to this sort of excess, but she knew this was her job now. After a long while, she had one final orgasm that resulted in only a few drops of sauce rather than the powerful squirts she had given before.

"Sorry boss, I'm tapped out. I need to recharge."

"That's okay, this should be enough to last us most of the day. If we run out of product, I can handle the storefront while you come back to the bakery to make some more."

Kim withdrew her fingers from herself and twisted around to kiss Heather. After some brief smooching and caressing, both women climbed of off the counter. They washed their hands and started gathering ingredients and utensils. Heather disappeared for a moment, then returned with a small plastic box filled with index cards.

"This is my recipe box. I remember every one of them by heart, but you'll need it for a while. Many of these recipes are rather conventional, but they all call for a certain amount of secret ingredient. Today, you're the boss. Pick out whichever recipes you like most. We'll make whatever you want to sell. Today will be the first day our customers eat your secret ingredient instead of mine."

"Thank you Heather, this means so much to me." Kim hugged her mentor tightly.

"Will you stay? To help me run the business, and to help me harvest the secret ingredient?"

"Of course I will, Kimberly."

Heather went around the bakery and turned all of the ovens on while Kim looked through the recipe cards. The two women worked together to make several batches of dough. Neither bothered to get dressed, and they both ended up with lots of flour on their nude bodies. Once everything was properly put into an oven, the new master baker and her mentor took a brief shower together in the employee bathroom and put on their work uniforms afterwards.

It wasn't long before the bakery was alive with the scents of cookies, cakes, pies, bread, and muffins. While waiting for the food to finish baking, Heather had Kim sign what documents didn't require a notary present. Ownership of the bakery would be fully signed over to her later that day.

As the various timers went off, Kimberly and Heather made their rounds transferring the baked goods from oven to cooling rack. Once everything was out of the heat, the women each took a cookie to sample. Kim's exquisite emissions brought a whole new world of flavor to a simple recipe. Both mentor and student were in awe of the result.

"Very well done Kimberly, our customers will love these!"

"I only hope we have enough for everyone!"

"Come on, we have to frost these cakes. It's opening time soon."

The bakers frosted and decorated and portioned everything neatly. Then, they transferred most of the freshly baked goodies to the storefront, with some reserve stock in the back. The store was soon ready to open, filled with fresh stock and wonderful smells. When finished, Kim and Heather still had a little while before they needed to open the store. They spent the extra time making out, having developed quite the bond during their morning of mutual pleasure.

The customers noticed the difference in Kimberly's flavor just as easily as Heather had. Sales increased dramatically, and word of mouth boosted the bakery's popularity further than ever before. Despite Heather's insistence that Kim change the name to Hong's Bakery, the name remained Dawson's as a sign of respect to the woman who had made it all happen. No matter how many times she was asked, Kimberly never sold her recipes for mass production or revealed her secret ingredient to the public.

3 THE SEED OF COURAGE

As a knight-errant of the silver order, my duty was to perform tasks unfitting of the king's armies. Sometimes, it meant settling petty disputes in rural villages. Sometimes, it meant slaying monsters, or escorting important people through dangerous territory. Depending on the situation, my job description could include anything from rescuing the princess to espionage and counter-espionage.

Today, it meant killing highly venomous bog-wolves and ripping their teeth out. King Aurum had been poisoned by a political rival, and now lay dying in the royal bedchamber. His would-be assassin, Duke Feron, attempted to take the throne while the king still lived. His treason was punished with a swift execution. This left me in the position of gathering ingredients for a cure to save the king's life.

There were not many female knight-errants aside from myself. Women were welcome to join the army and could earn any rank. Few, however, volunteered to be sent all over the kingdom for various miscellaneous tasks, staring death in the face one day and soul-crushing boredom the next. I did not regret my career choice, though I found myself wishing for more same-sex peers.

I considered myself fairly attractive, though some scars came with the lifestyle. I often kept my blonde hair trimmed short for comfort while wearing a helmet, though I sometimes allowed it to grow out. My muscle tone didn't take away from my femininity; it even enhanced some of my curves. I have always enjoyed dresses and lace, but rarely found the opportunity to wear such things. Protection was more important than fashion, always, and as such my typical attire consisted of steel plate and chain armor atop heavily padded garments. Unfortunately for me, bog-wolves had a knack for finding gaps in armor.

The king's life had been entrusted to a witch in his service, Mithesal. As the king's most trusted knight-errant, I was assigned to run errands for this woman. It was far easier to be enthusiastic about the assignment this morning, before a three-hour trudge through the swamp and numerous toxic wolf bites.

I began to feel quite woozy as I made my way down the castle corridor towards

Mithesal's laboratory. I had been able to ignore the venom's effects for a long while, but it grew stronger by the moment. After what seemed like an eternity, I reached the heavy oak door leading to Mithesal's lab.

I entered unannounced, Mithesal hardly looked up from her book. Her long, dark hair hung just past her shoulders. The garment she wore consisted of a long, wide strip of black silk wrapped around her body in asymmetrical patterns and tied off with a red ribbon. It roughly resembled a small dress, but left little to the imagination. It was common knowledge that she was far older than she appeared, though no one could say by how much. She looked to be in her early 20s, but she's been working at the castle since before I was born. I could admit that she was a rather attractive woman, but I have always held a natural distrust of magic users.

I removed a leather pouch filled with wolf teeth from my belt and held it out to the witch. "I gathered the bog-wolf fangs, as you asked."

"Excellent!" Mithesal sat her book aside and took the pouch from me. She dumped the teeth into a mortar, then handed me a glass bottle. "Drink that, it will rid you of the bog-wolf toxin."

I drank the potion without hesitation, wincing at the incredibly bitter taste of the herbal mixture. Mithesal cast a spell on me, healing my wounds. She then began to crush the wolf fangs and grind them up with a pestle.

"I hope you sent me wolf hunting for a reason, witch."

Mithesal glowered at me, she looked genuinely offended. "I would prefer you address me as Grand Enchantress Mithesal. If you cannot spare that much respect, Lady Amyle, you could at least address me by name. Furthermore, I serve the king just as you do. I would not endanger your life on a fool's errand, especially not while our king is on his deathbed."

"I apologize, Grand Enchantress Mithesal. I spoke out of turn."

"I accept your apology. I require two more ingredients before I can complete the cure, though."

"I am ready to aid you, we must hurry."

"Indeed we must. What I need next is dew from the petals of a pristine flower."

"There are many flowers in the grasslands, I will leave at once."

"Not just yet, Lady Amyle. I have been studying this pristine flower and I believe it to be figurative."

"Meaning?"

"We are not looking for a flower that grows from the ground. We are in need of a flower that lies between the legs. A flower that has not known the seed of a man."

My cheeks grew warm with a rosy blush. "My goodness, how lewd! Are you certain?"

"Quite. I also believe that your flower may be a suitable source of this dew. I have heard that the mighty Lady Amyle does not lie with men."

My blush grew deeper. "Where does one

hear a fool rumor like that?"

"From a tavern wench who seems to be rather well acquainted with you."

"All right, you speak truly. I have never been with a man. What do you need me to do?"

"Remove your armor, Lady Amyle. Clothing, too. Once you are fully nude, I will harvest your dew."

"Are you saying that you intend to masturbate me?"

"Yes. Would you prefer to do it yourself? It will be more fun if I help you."

I stood silently for a while, my face burning with embarrassment. "I would appreciate your touch, Grand Enchantress."

With much hesitation, I began to shed my armor. Once I was fully exposed, Mithesal embraced me from behind. Her experienced, knowing fingers teased my perky nipples. Just as I was beginning to relax, the touch stopped. I felt something cold touch my belly, and looked down to see a smooth stone rod. It was similar in shape to Mithesal's pestle, but wider and about eight inches long.

Mithesal slid the stone rod across my tummy, slowly pulling it along my flesh until the tip nestled between my moist folds. With short, deft strokes, she ground the cold stone against my pussy until I was good and wet for her. She knelt behind me and held a bowl in front of my pussy, then pushed the stone rod inside.

I clenched and gasped. The rod was quite thick, and uncomfortably cool. Mithesal pushed the toy deep into my nethers. She probed inward until I cried out. Having identified the depth limit for comfortable penetration, the witch began pumping the stone rod in and out of me enthusiastically.

The toy was naturally very smooth, just the slightest amount of my natural lubrication made the frantic inward thrusts come quite easily. My hips bucked beyond my ability to control them, I couldn't deny the pleasure this was giving me. The feeling only grew more intense when Mithesal's tongue began tickling my rear entrance.

My anus clenched, but her warm tongue coaxed it open. I'd never been licked there before, but the new feeling wasn't entirely unpleasant. My hot pussy warmed the stone rod over time. The warmer it became, the more pleasure it provided.

Mithesal changed her angle every few thrusts, making impossible for me to get used to her pattern. The more I relaxed, the faster she thrust the rod into me. My knees buckled, I held onto the edge of a table to support myself. It was all so much, I felt I was being driven mad with pleasure.

Before I could even realize how close I was, I slid headfirst into an earth-shattering climax. My back arched and I thrust my hips forward. A loud but brief scream escaped my lips. Several voluminous squirts of thick, clear, slippery lady honey burst from my loins to join my drippings in the bowl.

Mithesal didn't stop, despite my cries of protest. My oversensitive pussy couldn't handle this kind of torture! Squirming, bucking, shaking, screaming, I came again in just minutes. I glanced down at the bowl. I had provided quite a bit of fluid, but my juices were nowhere near the bowl's rim. Did Mithesal intend to fill it?

Not satisfied that she was getting me off quickly enough, Mithesal added magic to the mix. Her spell caused the rod to vibrate within me, bringing my ecstasy to a whole new level. I came again, harder than the first two times combined. It still was not enough, and the stone vibrator continued to pound away at my overstimulated pussy.

Mithesal just would not stop. My body began to feel both numb and oversensitized at the same time. I came again and again, yet still she tortured me. When the tenth orgasm came, my squirting caused the bowl to overflow. The vibration stopped, earning a sigh of relief from me. Mithesal teased me just a bit longer, then removed the stone rod.

Holding the bowl very carefully, Mithesal stood and placed the collected dew on a table. I happened to be leaning on that same table. My legs still felt too wobbly to stand. I only began to realize how wet my thighs felt when my senses came back to me.

"The only other ingredient I don't have is the seed of courage."

"I presume you speak not of a plant seed?"

"You presume correctly. Rather, we require the seed of a courageous warrior."

"Whose seed is most suitable in this

kingdom? I shall find him for you."

"Yours would be the most suitable, for you are more courageous than any man I know."

"But I am no man, I cannot give seed I do not have!"

Mithesal grabbed a vial from one of her racks and gave it to me. "Drink about half of this, it will solve our problems."

I eyed Mithesal warily, but did not question her judgment. The thick, white mixture inside the vial had a very salty, bitter taste. I wanted to wretch, but I managed to get it down. I handed the vial back, and soon after felt an odd tingle in my nethers.

The tingle grew stronger, making me squirm. It was most intense a couple of inches above my clit. I could feel a swelling and looked down to watch a new addition extend from my groin. My penis grew longer and thicker by the second. Once it reached its maximum size, the foreskin peeled back to reveal the engorged glans. The skin between my penis and vagina grew very loose, and then a pair of testicles dropped.

"By the gods, what sort of magic is this?"

"Dragon semen, powdered silver, and several varieties of phallic mushroom." Mithesal picked up another bowl and embraced me from behind again. "Now, let's collect that seed so I can finish the elixir."

"Must I fill this bowl as well?"

"No, only a small sample of the seed of courage is required."

The witch grabbed ahold of my cock and

began jacking me off without further ado. I hissed through my teeth at the intense new feeling. Each stroke pulled my foreskin back and forth across the incredibly sensitive tip of my member. I had never realized how soft Mithesal's hands were until that moment, her touch was heavenly.

The witch did not take her time with this task. Her hand moved in swift, confident strokes with a focus solely on making me cum. I squirmed uncomfortably, entirely new to this sensation. It was only a few short, but intense, minutes before I lost control and cried out. Several ropes of sticky white spunk coated the inside of the bowl.

Mithesal sat the bowl aside and moved to kneel in front of me. She pulled back my foreskin and took my cock into her mouth, earning a loud gasp from me. She suckled and licked my much too sensitive organ, taking the last few drops of my load into her mouth. Just as I was about to beg her to stop, she pulled away.

I found an empty spot on one of Mithesal's tables and pulled myself up to sit for a spell. While I rested, Mithesal resumed grinding the wolf fangs into powder. She then mixed the powder with my feminine emissions. Next she added my male slime, and a few herbal powders. Once the musky mixture was finished, she cautiously poured it into a bottle and inserted a cork stopper.

"It is done, we may now purify the king's body."

"Hold on. How are we to be rid of this?" I gestured towards my penis."

"It will disappear easily enough. You need only put your seed inside a woman, and it will vanish."

"I do not wish to face the king while I am of both sexes. Grand Enchantress Mithesal, may I put my seed in you so that I can resume my natural form?"

"I will allow this, but only on one condition. If you are to ravish me, I would like to ravish you afterward."

"Fair enough, you have a deal."

Mithesal tugged at the red ribbon that held her clothing on. The instant it came loose, the entire garment fell to the floor. She gestured for me to get down from where I was, then took my place on the table. She leaned back slightly, legs spread wide. I admired her beautiful form, a naturally lovely body further enhanced by magic.

"Take me, Lady Amyle. As swiftly or as easily as you please, I am not a picky woman."

I approached, rather nervous, and rubbed the tip of my penis against her moist slit. She was quite aroused already, I assume from the sexual tortures she had previously put me through. I eased my way inside with a long groan. The tight, gripping heat overwhelmed my recently grown meat with indescribably intense sensations.

My hips bucked forward on reflex, burying the rest of my shaft within her wet embrace with a single push. I began to thrust immediately, haphazardly slapping my groin against hers with no semblance of rhythm or restraint. I couldn't control myself, and I wouldn't be able to take her gently even if I wanted to.

Mithesal wrapped her legs around my waist and raked her sharp fingernails down my back. The closeness of this position had our bare breasts pressing together. Every little movement ground my stiff nipples against hers, the sensation sent chills up and down my spine. Her sensual moans only served to turn me on even more.

Mere seconds later, I came. With one last brutal thrust, I buried myself in Mithesal and screamed. Feminine fluids splattered the inside of my thighs and the back of my balls, while at the same instant, my masculine fluids shot deep into Mithesal's pussy. Just as the witch had said, my penis shrank and disappeared back inside me after my orgasm. I stroked the patch of skin where it had been, appreciating my return to smoothness.

When I turned my attention back to Mithesal, she was already drinking the rest of the white potion. Her reaction wasn't as strong as mine, I assume she's used to this sort of thing. The effect was much the same though, a penis and testicles sprouted from her loins. Her shaft was not quite as long as mine had been, but was somewhat thicker.

"Bend over," Mithesal instructed. "Hands on the table, I want to take you standing."

I positioned myself as asked, leaning forward and pushing my butt out. Mithesal slid her plump organ between my legs, teasing my pussy with it. Her intimidating girth gave me pause, but I had given her my word so I said nothing. I shut my eyes tight and waited. I was already quite wet, but the grinding had more of my aroused slime trickling out.

The head of Mithesal's wide cock parted my folds, then a rough thrust buried half of her length in a single push. I gasped sharply, but the discomfort was not as great as I had expected. After the thorough workout the witch had given me earlier, my pussy was extremely wet and also quite relaxed.

Mithesal ravished me hard and fast. Whether she was returning the favor or taking revenge, I wasn't sure. Such rough sex with such a thick penis did certainly hurt, but it also felt incredibly good at the same time. Her thrusts into me were not as swift as mine into her, but she was also able to maintain a steady pace that I had not.

Her soft hands roamed my body. From my hips, she slid up to caress along my abs, then down my sides and up my back, where she gripped my shoulders. She gave me a few particularly hard thrusts, then pulled out.

Before I could ask if she'd finished, I felt the end of that huge member poke my puckered anus. My asshole clenched up reflexively, but she shoved her way inside anyway. I screamed, having never taken anything more than a tongue in my ass before. Her hands moved to my breasts, and she thankfully took a more slow and easy approach to my backside than she'd used on my vagina.

Those magic fingers teased my nipples far more exquisitely than they had before. The pleasure in my breasts helped to offset the pain in my ass a little. One of my own hands migrated down to stroke my clit. While I was distracted with pleasure, I barely noticed her speeding up a little at a time.

Soon, the witch was pounding me at a reasonably swift pace, her hips slapping my firm rump. Just as I was starting to enjoy the feeling of being fucked in the ass, Mithesal came. Her orgasmic vocalizations sounded to me like the voice of an angel. The amount of cum she packed into my backside was astonishing, I wouldn't have though such a productive climax to even be possible.

That thick cock shrank and vanished just as mine had. I suddenly felt empty, save for the wet warmth of her cum. Sticky white seed drooled out of my gaping bottom, running down my thighs in streams. I clenched again and again until I had closed myself up a bit, then started getting dressed. It took Mithesal far longer to put her clothes on than it had taken to remove them.

"Before we deliver the elixir to the king, I've a question for you."

"Of course."

"Your seed is in me. Does that mean my flower is no longer pristine?"

"I ejaculated in your backside, so your lovely flower remains pristine."

"We must do this again some time."

"Come to my lab any time. If I am not busy with something, I would be happy to pleasure you. Though, if we use too much of my hermaphrodite potion, I may need to send you to collect more of the key ingredient.

My eyes went wide at the thought of what collecting dragon semen might entail. I pushed the distracting idea from my mind, though. There were more important matters to deal with. Mithesal finished putting on her wrap and grabbed the elixir. We left together to present the cure to the king.

.

4 FULLY MOONED

Green lipstick mingled with my red, making a smeared mess on my face and hers. My lover's tongue writhed in my mouth, as strong in its movements as she was skilled in its use. I broke away to take a breath, but her lips pressed back to mine insistently.

Tess and I had been girlfriends since middle school, and we were now enjoying our late twenties together. I ran my fingers through her dark hair, cut to shoulder length and straightened. A bright green accent stripe was dyed into her bangs. Green was her favorite color, and she made sure everyone knew. She had an afro when we met, but had been straightening her hair since freshman year of high school. Her new style looked good, but there were times when I missed the old look.

My hands caressed her smooth mocha skin, warm and bare. I sometimes called her my chocolate princess, but she always gave me the strangest look when I said that. Her body was incredible to look upon: curvaceous yet understated, busty but reasonably so, athletic but not bulky. She perched upon the line between above-average and Hollywood-beautiful with her round, squeezable ass.

I myself wasn't bad looking, though I considered my figure inferior to hers. My body was considerably softer; I was even beginning to get a belly. I wasn't chubby by any reasonable standard, but I didn't have that same balance of body fat and muscle tone that made her look so amazing. My arms were a little more toned than I wanted them to be, while the rest of me was squishy. I refused to get a tan, lest my pale Irish skin burn to a crisp. She said she liked my alabaster complexion, but I seethed with envy every time I saw a woman with a nice tan. My boobs were significantly larger than hers. A bit too big, even. Having natural F-cups in a town of small to medium busts meant I had to special order most of my bras and tops.

My hair was one point of pride. Shampooed and conditioned to a high sheen, bleached and dyed blonde, straightened and meticulously styled every morning in a well-practiced brushing pattern; my glorious golden mane came to about mid-way on my back. I was afraid to bleach and dye my eyebrows, though. Two strips of coppery-red hair revealed my natural color to the world. My eyes were a deep emerald green, one of Tess's favorite things about me.

Tess suddenly broke out of the incredible kiss with a gasp. "The moon is supposed to be full tonight! I completely forgot!"

I tried to look concerned, even though I was actually kind of annoyed. She always made a point of avoiding me on the night of the full moon. "What's wrong?" "Nothing, but you need to go home, Ashley. I don't want anything to happen." "What's going to happen?"

"Hopefully nothing. I'll see you tomorrow."

"Tess, you know you can trust me. If there's something going on, you can tell me."

She hesitated for a long moment, avoiding eye contact. Finally, she spoke. "Ashley, I'm a werewolf. I've been trying to protect you from that side of me. It's so much harder to control myself when the moon is full, I'm afraid I'll hurt you." I stared at Tess, blown away by the ridiculousness of what she'd just said. "Look, if you're not going to take me seriously…"

"It's true! Every time the light of the full moon touches my skin, I turn into a big wolf!"

"Bullshit."

"I am telling you the truth! When have I ever lied to you about anything? I wouldn't tell you something like this if I didn't mean it!"

"Tess, honey, werewolves aren't real. I can believe that you believe this, but it just isn't true."

"I just don't want to hurt you."

45

"Then close the blinds, maybe? You said moonlight has to touch your skin, right? We shouldn't have to put our relationship on hold based on the lunar cycle."

"I agree, I just..." she sighed. "I guess you're right, closing the blinds should keep it from happening. It's supposed to be cloudy tonight, too, so we might be okay."

"That's more like it! Now give me some loving, my chocolate princess!"

Tess frowned and crossed her arms. "You've really got to stop saying that."

"I'm sorry, is it racist?"

"A little bit. It's mostly just dumb. I think you can do better than that."

Tess stood and shut her window blinds, dimming the red-gold rays of sunset shining through the window. A few slivers of light still made it onto the bed. She looked at the little streaks of sunlight with a worried expression, chewing her lower lip.

"Stop worrying, you aren't going to change."

"I'm just trying to keep you safe."

"Even if you do turn into a wolf tonight, don't you love me? You aren't going to become so feral that you forget what we mean to each other, are you?"

"I don't know. I never remember anything that happens in wolf form, I just wake up, and everything around me is chewed and clawed and smashed to pieces. If I change, just run away. It's best not to chance it. I couldn't live with myself if I hurt you. If you can't get out of the house, there's a handgun in the study hidden behind some books on the left side of the top shelf. I keep it loaded."

"Is it loaded with silver bullets?"

"No."

"Then what good will that do me?"

"I'm pretty sure that part is a myth."

"You transform into a wolf because of moonlight, but silver bullets are a myth?"

I must have hit a nerve, because she suddenly became livid. It had been a very long time since she'd shouted at me. "You don't have to live with this, I do. If you don't respect me enough to accept the warning I'm trying to give you, then you can go back to your own damn house and wait until I'm ready to see you again. If you don't believe me, that's fine, but don't you dare lie there and mock me."

"I'm sorry Tess, I didn't mean anything by it! That was a dumb thing for me to say, I shouldn't have said it. I can see this means a lot to you, and I was wrong to make fun of it."

Tess sighed. "It's all right, just don't do it again. I'm sorry I yelled at you. I'd just hate to wake up tomorrow and find what's left of you on the floor, peeled like a banana."

I cocked a brow. "You've thought about this."

"I have nightmares about this. I'm terrified that the savage beast inside me will harm the one I love most."

"You'd never hurt me Tess, I know you wouldn't."

"How I envy your confidence."

"Come back to bed, forget all this wolf

stuff tonight. We'll have a big werewolf discussion tomorrow."

"But..."

I spread my legs. The black and white stripes on my thigh socks led her eyes along my legs, directly to my glistening pink. "Don't you want to make love to your human bitch, miss big bad wolf?"

Tess smiled, finally. "Now that is a pet name I like."

She got back in bed and crawled towards me on all fours, like an animal. She touched her nose to mine and growled playfully. I tried my best not to laugh. Still, as silly as this all felt, it was also kind of hot.

My lover mounted me, squishing our tits together and mashing her crotch against mine. I angled my hips to help her find my glistening petals with hers. Once contact had been made, she started humping. We were both quite wet already, and our slippery snatches slid against each other quite easily. The muff on muff contact had me writhing and moaning.

I wrapped my arms around her, but she grabbed them and pinned my wrists to the bed behind my head. She had to sit up a little to hold my arms down, which put an end to the delightful booby-squishage but allowed me to watch her tits bounce while she humped me. I could see a gleam in her eye: this wolf-play thing was really turning her on. I wondered if her weirdness on the full moon all this time had been an elaborate set-up for some role-play. Were that the case, I could play along.

"Oh Miss Wolf, such pretty eyes you have!"

"All the better to watch those fat tits bounce, my sexy Irish bitch. And you can call me Big Bad."

"Oh Big Bad, what graceful arms you have."

"All the better to hold you down with while I take you, my vision in alabaster."

"Oh Big Bad, what an amazing tongue you have!"

Tess leaned in and licked my cheek. "All the better to taste you with, my scrumptious Oreo cream."

I gave Tess a weird look. "Scrumptious Oreo cream?"

She looked surprised, but didn't break her rhythm. "What? Is that racist?"

"I don't know. I don't think so. It's mostly just weird. Though maybe it would make sense if we had another black girl join us, with me in the middle."

"If you ask me again to invite my sister to join us, I swear..."

"Well now that you say that, I won't."

Tess smacked her pussy against mine particularly hard, making me yelp. She went right back to grinding afterward, but neither of us said anything else. Every time I got close, she would back off for a few seconds. The teasing was fun at first, but then it just started to annoy me. I watched the light grow dimmer and dimmer, wondering how long she was going to delight in my torture.

"Tess, let me finish!"

"What's the magic word?"

"Please, let me cum!"

"Okay, since you asked so nicely."

Tess moved her hips faster. When I got close this time, she didn't pull away. I wrapped my legs around her waist and shuddered. Her teasing had driven me to an unusually wet climax, I made a slippery mess all over her crotch. She came soon after, letting out a quiet groan and adding to our collective slipperiness.

I kissed my ebony lover on the lips, silently thanking her for the pleasant ride with some shameless tonguing. She released my hands, and I moved them to stroke her naked back. Her tongue wiggled against mine while I tasted the back of her teeth.

Suddenly, Tess broke away from the kiss with a sharp grunt. She tried to pull away from me, so I let her go. She sat up on her knees and put her face in her hands, then cried out.

"Tess, what's wrong? Are you hurt?"

My girlfriend's beautiful, nude body began to change before my very eyes. Her fingers grew longer, and her nails narrowed into short claws. Her feet got bigger, and the arches flattened out. Her ears stretched and moved, sliding further up the side of her head and becoming very pointy. They changed shape until they looked just like dog ears.

With the sounds she was making, Tess was either in tremendous pain or about to have a really good orgasm. A splash of feminine fluids hit the bed to clear things up. Her face changed next. Tess's lips and nose both grew longer, eventually fusing together. The hideous mess of face-flesh gradually shaped into a canine muzzle. Her lovely breasts shrank and disappeared into her chest. Then, thick black fur started to sprout all over her body.

I wanted to run away like she'd told me to, but I couldn't move. I was simultaneously mystified and terrified watching her change. When the changes were complete, she just sat there and stared at me for a while. The warm, brown eyes I had fallen in love with were now a bestial, reflective gold. Neither of us moved for the first few minutes.

I noticed something on the edge of my vision and looked down. My eyes went wide in astonishment. At some point during her transformation, Tess had sprouted a set of testicles and a bright red canine cock. That was certainly new! I recognized the shape from one of the toys she used on me sometimes, though the silicone dick wasn't nearly as large as this thing. It had to be at least eight inches long and looked as thick as my wrist. The impressive knot at the base was just slightly thicker than the shaft itself.

Tess's wolf boner swayed from side to side as I stared at it. I realized all too late that the wolf had started moving towards me the moment I broke eye contact. He was right in my face before I knew it, his cold black nose touching mine. A splash of color grabbed my attention. I glanced slightly to the left and noticed that the werewolf still had Tess's accent stripe. I was sure that streak of dyed green fur would be the last thing I ever saw.

The wolf's muzzle opened and a long, thick tongue lashed across my lips. I opened my mouth in surprise, and ended up getting French-kissed by a werewolf. His tongue was longer than anything I could imagine. I gagged when he tried to throat-kiss me. While we were making out, his big strong hands roamed across my naked body. His fingertips and the heel of his palm had smooth black pads that were hairless, but the rest of his hand had a coat of soft, warm fur. I stroked him as well, running my fingers though that lovely dark fluff.

After an hour or so, the wolf got bored of making me suck his tongue and instead started licking my tits. I slid one of my legs up and used my toes to feel around between his legs. I thought maybe Tess still had a pussy somewhere, but this wolf was all male. He growled when my socked foot touched the back of his balls. I couldn't tell if it was an angry sound or a lusty one, but I decided not to risk it and moved my foot away.

The werewolf tortured my stiff nipples for what felt like an eternity, dragging that washcloth-sized tongue over my sensitive flesh again and again. Just when I began thinking I was about to have my first breast orgasm, the licking stopped. Tess moved further down my body, until his furry head was between my legs. The first lick was long and slow. He parted my folds with his tongue and licked from one end of my slit to the other. I humped his muzzle throughout the duration, and very nearly climaxed.

After that, the licks came swiftly. The way he lapped at my snatch with his huge tongue sounded like a thirsty dog drinking. He held my thighs in his strong hands and chowed down on my pussy. I could see his big, bushy tail wagging in the air. It didn't take me long at all to cum, and my lupine lover eagerly lapped up my sweet fluids. He tried to pull away, but I grabbed his cheek ruffs and held him in place. The werewolf obediently resumed licking my snatch, and I couldn't help but to hump his face.

I came a second, then a third time. After licking me to completion that third time, the wolf growled. I released his face from my grasp and he sat up on his knees. Still holding my thighs, he pulled me further down the bed until his cock laid between my legs. Watching it throb and drool on my lower tummy like that really hammered home just how big he was.

"Whoa, no! That is not going to fit! Down boy!"

My protests were ignored. The wolf lined himself up and shoved his way inside. The pointy chisel-tip nudged my folds open and pierced into my tight pink quite easily. It helped that I was incredibly wet at that point, and that he was leaking precum like a broken faucet. He kept going until his knot slipped inside me, the tip of his cock pressed right up against the opening of my cervix. I was wrong, not only had he fit but I was the perfect size to take all of him.

Having proven his point, the wolf pulled almost all the way out of me. Then he shoved back in, hard. He did it over and over, taking me in slow brutal thrusts that utilized the full length of his cock. I grunted every time he plowed into me. He was going much too deep for comfort, but it was kind of turning me on. I knew I'd regret doing this in the morning, but I could get into it now.

The wolf's knot grew a little bit bigger with each thrust. It would stretch me wide on the way in, than stretch me wider on the way out. I could hear a soft, wet pop each time he tugged it out of me. It actually started to get quite large, and hurt a little on the way in or out.

After a certain point, the wolf couldn't plunge his knot into me very easily, my little pussy just put up too much resistance for his girth. He switched from the slow and hard thrusts to quick, frantic humping. I cried out in mixed pleasure and pain. His growing knot slapped my pussy with each slam, I was certain he'd end up bruising me like this. About a minute later, he switched his strategy again. The werewolf now took me in short, very hard bucks. Just when I began to wonder the purpose, my pussy gave way and his swollen knot popped in. I screamed and came, squirting into his fur with a painful orgasm.

With his knot inside, the wolf jerked his

hips back and forth hard and fast. His pubic fur tickled my clit, and his knot stroked my g-spot with every little movement. I came again in seconds. My orgasmic squeezing helped his knot reach its full size, swollen, until it was bigger than my fist.

With just one more push, the werewolf threw his head back and howled. Hot wolf semen squirted directly into my womb. The warm heat made me gasp. With each throb, his cock gave another spurt of burning-hot wolf cum. His muzzle found my lips again, and we resumed our interspecies make-out session.

Later that night, I still lay in bed, bored and sore. Tess was still on top of me, holding me close and wagging his tail. His dick was still stuck inside me, like I was his little bitch. It had stopped being fun after-play a while ago, and now it was just a waiting game.

After a seeming eternity, Tess's knot shrank and he pulled out of me. His cum was thin and watery, and it ran out of my thoroughly abused cunt like a river. I glanced over at the bedside clock, 10:53. We had been stuck like that for forty-eight minutes and he'd been ejaculating the entire time.

Tess moved between my legs and eagerly lapped at my sore pussy. I winced every time he licked me. His rough entry when tying the knot had left me a little bruised. I scratched behind his ears while he licked up his own mess, content to let him clean me so that I could keep at least some of his stuff off of my clothes.

I kept an eye on the clock as well though, and when it got to be 11:00, I pushed him away. I stood and stretched, then made my way over to the pile of clothes on the floor and bent down. I hadn't thought my actions through, and didn't consider that I was mooning a werewolf. Just as I grasped my panties, Tess's strong werewolf hands grasped my waist. With a single, hard thrust, he buried the entire length of his fat dick in my ass.

"Ow, not there! Tess, you've got the wrong hole! Take it out, take it out!"

He ignored me once more and began thrusting, hard and fast. His cock was coated in a mixture of both our sexual fluids, which made it nice and slick. If not for that, I'm sure he would have ripped me apart. With every thrust, his furry pelvis smacked my ass, and his big wolf balls impacted my aching pussy. I could feel my butt jiggle while he fucked me and made a mental note to start taking the stairs instead of the elevator.

I could hear Tess snarling in pure carnal ecstasy. He was definitely enjoying this more than I was. Despite how much it hurt to be brutally sodomized by a werewolf, I couldn't deny that it was starting to feel good to me too. Some quiet moans mixed their way in with my pained grunts. Those heavy nuts pounding my pussy started to get me pretty worked up, too.

I had actually begun to enjoy myself, until I felt those short and hard thrusts again.

"No no no no no! Bad Tess! Bad werewolf! Do not stick your knot in my ass! You can't tie with me there!"

Once again, my protests were useless. He forced his knot up into my tight asshole, and I screamed. His knot ballooned out to fist size again, but it felt even bigger in my back door than it had felt in the front. He howled, and started filling me up like a car with bad mileage.

I stood there, fully bent with my hands on the floor and a wolf cumming in my rectum. I grit my teeth, disturbed by the idea of staying like this for as long as the first time. I was saved, however, by cloud cover. The moonlight had been dimmed by the blinds, but enough still got through to fill the room with pale blue-silver light. Once the clouds rolled in, Tess's bedroom became pitch-black.

The flow of wolf seed stopped immediately, Tess's cock shrank and disappeared in seconds. Her hands got smaller as well, returning to the milky-smooth human hands I was used to. The noises she was making during her transformation became steadily more human. I couldn't see her in the darkness, but I knew she was herself again when all I felt pressed against my ass was smooth skin and a little patch of trimmed bush. Her hands slid around my hips, ass, and back.

"Ashley?"

"Present."

"Oh my god! I don't remember a thing! I'm so sorry, did I hurt you?" "You hurt my butt a little, but I'll be okay."

"What do you mean? Did I bite you?"

"You fucked me up the ass and shoved your knot into me."

"I...what? How is that even possible? I don't have a knot!"

"You turned into a male werewolf when you transformed. I don't know if you do that every time, but you had a knotted dick as big as my arm."

"I've never actually seen myself in wolf form, but I know I'm not a man-wolf."

"You came in me!"

"Bullshit." Tess moved away from me me and felt around for the light switch. I stood up straighter and put my hands on my hips, waiting. We both winced when the light came on, but then she looked at the tiny streams of cum running down my thighs, and the steady drip from my savaged butthole. "Oh my god, I did cum in you!"

"Yes, a lot! Your wolf form has a hell of a tongue, though. He's not a bad lay, either, I just don't care much for tying with him."

"Why didn't you run away? I could have really hurt you! We may not be so lucky, next time."

"I may have to get you to rim me, next time." I gave Tess a big hug and a kiss on the lips, then started getting dressed. "Thanks for the great time, but I have work in the morning, so I need to skedaddle. Love you, baby."

"Love you too." Tess kissed me back, then eyed the trail of semen leading from the bed to me. "I'd better clean that up before it dries. See you tomorrow?"

"Count on it." We hugged again, and I made my way out while she got a washcloth. After that, she never avoided me when the moon was full. Getting her wolfy rocks off curbed the destructive behaviors she was so afraid of. She showed me the steel shed she used to lock herself in, and all of the scratches and dents in the walls. Getting some pussy kept the wolf in her calm, and I was happy to help. In time, I got used to taking the knot and even enjoyed it. I learned to get off on anal as well, and after a few sessions with wolf-Tess I even enjoyed taking that fat knot up my butt. Cloud cover rarely interrupted her transformations, so I often had to get bred and knotted in both holes numerous times before she became herself again. She would keep going until sunrise on a clear night. I always had a full month to recover in between wolf-matings, though, so I could deal with getting pounded raw like that. My knowledge of her dark secret brought the two of us closer together than ever. One year after my first time seeing Tess in wolf-form, she proposed.

5 GETTING SLAID

A long, winding path stretched before me. I had been walking for hours and still had some ways to go. My destination was an old temple built into the mountainside. A walkway had been cut into the stone in centuries past, but it had long since fallen into disuse. Scraggly weeds crept over the edges of the path.

My armor added a metallic sound to each step I took—strong steel plate designed to ward off physical attacks and enchanted to resist fire. My shield was fire-resistant as well, and my sword carried strong enchantments to enhance its cutting power and durability. There were few warriors with the courage to face a dragon in single combat, and those of us who did so took such precautions.

At last I reached the golden dragon's domain. I drew my blade and raised my shield, then advanced slowly. The people of a nearby village had put a bounty on the creature's head. Though it had yet to cause any harm, they feared it for its presence alone. Given that dragons rarely lived in peaceful coexistence with anything else, I believed their fears to be well founded.

The ancient temple lay in ruins, collapsed after centuries of negligence and overgrown with wispy vines. My visored helmet limited my field of vision, but my senses were sharp. Few rooms were left intact, and I searched each one.

Finally, I came upon the beast's lair. A pile of broken stone and metal furniture lay just outside the doorway. The largest of the intact rooms had been redecorated in a sense. A hole had been torn in the ceiling to form a crude skylight, with the basin of a large fountain dragged underneath to catch rainwater. Unlit torches lined the walls, though they all had fresh burn marks. In one corner sat a pile of trinkets and treasure. In the adjacent corner was a pile of cushions and blankets, upon which the dragon rested.

Bright golden scales covered most of her body. Her underside was a pale beige color and her eyes were brilliant blue. She lay sprawled out on her back, eyeing me warily. She took a long drag from a hookah and then blew smoke from her nose.

"A visitor, hmm? Had I known a shiny tin man was coming to visit, I'd have baked a cake. Why don't you put down that big knife and come share my smoke?"

"I am here at the behest of the village of

Trian to slay you, foul beast."

The dragoness furrowed her brow and brought her free paw to her chest. "Foul? I take umbrage to that, sir knight! I assure you my scent is most inoffensive!"

"I believe you have done nothing wrong, and, Lord help me, I don't care. I was offered a good bit of gold to slay you, and I shall."

"A mercenary? How frightening! Whatever pittance those ignorant dirt farmers are paying you, I'll double it if you let me live."

I glanced over at her treasure hoard. She wasn't as wealthy as some of the dragons I had slain, but she could easily cover her offer and then some. I weighed my options carefully. If I killed her, I could take everything. However, I had also learned the hard way that the more relaxed dragons tended to be, the more powerful they are as well. The last time I had fought a dragon with a sense of humor, I had very nearly died.

After some consideration, I sheathed my sword. "You have a deal, dragon. I will accept your payment of treasure and leave you be."

"Oh good, I detest violence. The last warrior who tried to take my head left such a mess. I was afraid I'd never get the floor clean."

While I couldn't be certain of the truth in her words, I did feel that I'd made the right decision. I hadn't brought a pack or satchel with me, and I had to improvise. I removed my shield and piled treasure onto it like a tray. I counted out double the value the villagers had offered, with as much of a tip as I thought I could get away with. I hefted the now-heavy shield and began to leave, but the dragon's voice halted me.

"Wait, you don't have to leave just yet. I haven't had any male company in a long while. You are a man under all of that armor, right?"

"Yes, I am indeed a man."

"Good, good. I sometimes have trouble distinguishing with humans. It's even harder when you cover yourselves in metal. Do you think I'm pretty?"

In truth, I'd never thought of such a thing. I looked over her form again, now checking her out instead of sizing her up. The hard golden scales on much of her body were sleek and shiny. Her underside looked soft and smooth compared to the rest of her. The dragoness had a curvy, slender figure and a long, narrow tail. With the way she was lying down, I could easily see her genital slit.

"Your form is rather appealing for a dragon. I have never thought of your kind in such a way, but I could call you pretty."

"Oh, thank you, sir knight." The dragoness reached down and spread her scaly beige outer labia open to expose her glistening pinkness to me. "Would you like to thrust a different kind of sword into me?"

I stared at the dragon's vagina, stunned by her proposition. "You would mate with a human?"

"It's been so long since I've been penetrated by anything, save for my own tail. Truthfully, I would mate with anyone that would have me. Why don't you shed your metal skin and have a little fun with me?"

"I would not do such a thing with a dragon. I am sorry."

The golden dragon laughed. "That is no trouble. My kind has many powers. Observe."

She changed before my very own eyes. Her body shrank and her scales smoothed into flesh. She became a voluptuous human woman with luxuriant golden blonde hair and a slight tan. "Is this figure more to your liking, sir knight? Come and share the pleasures of the human body with me."

My gut told me this was a trap. However, my codpiece was becoming uncomfortably tight and its occupant demanded that I accept the dragon-lady's offer. Against my better judgment, I laid down my shield and began to remove my armor. The dragoness looked on with growing interest as I exposed more of myself to her. In time I stood amidst a pile of steel, my flesh exposed. I had on nothing but boots, though she stopped me when I tried to remove them.

"Leave the boots on; they're sexy."

I made my way over to her recumbent form, my half-mast penis swaying with each step. Once I stood before the pile of cushions, I knelt. With my thumbs, I spread her slit open and got a nice up-close look. I took an experimental lick and found her flavor pleasing. The tongue tricks that got tavern wenches screaming seemed to work equally well on this shape shifter. Her anatomy was, after all, basically identical now. Her pink pearl was thicker than the end of my pinky, and I teased it relentlessly.

The dragon-lady ran her nails through my hair and humped my face. Her sweet juices flowed freely, making a slippery mess of her crotch. Once she was wet enough, I dragged two fingers through the moisture drooling from her crevice and then firmly inserted them. She tossed her head back and let out a husky moan.

I vigorously pumped my fingers in and out of her twat, prodding her G-spot with every push. She was remarkably tight and was far hotter inside than any normal woman. Her being stretched around my digits made my penis ache with need. My tongue tortured her stiff clit in every way I knew how.

My comely blonde lover trembled; I could tell she was fighting hard to hold back. Her willpower didn't hold out forever, though. Soon enough, she held my face tight to her crotch and screamed. A tiny puff of flame burst from her lips, and a rush of sweet fluids flooded from her pussy. I enthusiastically licked up her flavorful muff sauce. After riding out her afterglow, she released me from her grasp.

"Thank you, sir knight! You are quite a

talented lover."

"I am no knight, just a common sell-sword. Call me Sergei."

"Very well, Sergei. You may call me Quelaana."

She eyed my erection hungrily when I stood. "Are you prepared for what comes next, Quelaana?"

She grinned. "I think you have more than adequately prepared me. I am ready. Though I did not know humans could grow so large. This will be quite a ride."

I mounted my lover and wedged the head of my thick cock between her folds. With a single hard push, I buried my full length within her. She gasped and clenched tight. I waited until she relaxed, then pulled back and began to buck swiftly. Quelaana raked her nails down my back, moaning deeply.

Her hands slid lower in their tender caress. I felt a finger poke my anus and clenched reflexively. I ignored the tickle there and focused on breeding the bronze-skinned beauty. A moment later, she pressed her finger inside me. I stopped my thrusting with a grunt, feeling her slender digit wiggle deeper inside me.

"You're a nasty one, Quelaana."

"Who said you could stop thrusting?"

I resumed humping the dragon-lady, trying to ignore the uncomfortable sensation in my formerly virginal backside. The tip of her naughty finger found my prostate, earning a gasp from me. She teased my sensitive gland with quick strokes of her fingertip.

My hips swiveled faster, pounding away at her burning-hot snatch. My thick cock pierced her again and again. I could clearly hear the lewd, squishy sounds of wet sex and it further fueled my arousal. The prostate stimulation felt strange, but it was having an effect. I could already tell I wouldn't be able to last long like this.

I gritted my teeth and concentrated, intent to make Quelaana cum before letting myself go. Fortunately, I didn't have to wait long. She soon threw her head back and screamed again, letting out another puff of flame in the process. Her pussy clenched up around me and splashed my groin with hot pussy juice. The orgasmic contractions were enough to finish me off. I thrust deep and let out a roar of triumph. My thick white seed painted her insides. She timed her clenches and kept up the prostate massage to milk me for every last drop.

Once I was spent, I remained inside her. She stroked my back and I rubbed her sides. We rested there and caressed each other for a long while, basking in a mutual afterglow. After some time, she removed her finger from my bottom. I pulled my softening cock out of her pussy and rolled onto the pile of cushions next to her. Quelaana turned back into a dragon and kissed me with her long, snake-like tongue. Then, she curled up with me in a close cuddle.

"Sergei, I have a request to ask of you."

"I'm listening."

"Stay with me. Be my lover and my protector. Keep me safe from those that would do me harm. Keep me warm at night."

"What's in it for me?"

"I will make love to you every night, in any way you choose. I'll also share my treasure hoard with you; any treasure I acquire will also be yours."

I grinned. "How could I possibly resist an offer like that? I accept. I will be your mate and your bodyguard."

"Thank you, my handsome and virile dragon knight."

"Dragon knight?"

"In olden times, a human warrior who served a dragon both sexually and otherwise was known as a dragon knight. To my knowledge, the title has not been used in some time. I think you are the first dragon knight in centuries."

"Dragon Knight Sergei, I like the sound of that…."

"As do I, my rugged human lover."

The villagers were not happy with my betrayal, but they were wrong to want to kill such a beautiful creature in the first place. Others came to fight her, but we fought them off together. Our combined power was enough to ward off any attacker. At first motivated by sex and treasure, I learned to love Quelaana in time.

No longer was I a nondescript adventurer for hire. Though society at large shunned me for loving a dragon, I became a figure of legend—Dragon Knight Sergei, stalwart defender and devoted mate of the golden dragon Quelaana.

6 GIRLY

The soft hiss of plastic sliding across metal hit my ears every couple of seconds. Skirt after skirt drifted by my vision, all of them were pretty but I'd yet to see one that truly wowed me. This store had an excellent selection and a wide variety of patterns, but most of the skirts in my size just didn't fit my style.

Long mahogany hair dangled down my back, a perfect match to my brown eyes. My slender fingers ended in delicately manicured nails, painted purple. A pair of glossy black pumps cradled my small, delicate feet. Slim, graceful legs clad in stockings rose up to disappear beneath a gray tartan miniskirt. My top was a white-buttoned blouse, with the first few buttons undone. It fit a bit loosely on my flat chest, but it was comfortable and breathed well. Despite my skinniness, my butt still had some substance and formed a nicely squeezable heart shape when I bent over. My hips were my greatest point of pride, though—truly succulent curves that looked good no matter what I wore. Still, selectiveness isn't a personality trait that I particularly mind.

After some searching, I came upon a skirt I liked—white, with smoky black swirls. The material was soft and smooth, I spent a moment stroking it. Just as I'd taken it from the rack, Nicole snuck up on me and pinched my ass.

My sexy, blonde girlfriend had quite a few things picked out for herself. She and I wore the same size and had about the same figure, but she wasn't quite so picky as I was. We looked nearly alike, save for the difference in hair and eye color—oh, and those luscious melons of hers. She could definitely fill out a top better than I. An orange camisole left her cleavage mostly exposed, while a khaki short skirt covered her lovely rump. Her feet were wrapped in a pair of brown leather sandals, she loved to show off her toes. Her toenails were painted different colors: red on the big toe of each foot, then orange, then yellow, then green, and finally blue on both little toes to form a rainbow excluding indigo and violet.

"I found a top that might fit you," said Nicole. I stopped staring at her feet and looked into her lovely green eyes. "I think it will even match that pretty skirt you've picked out."

She handed me a sleeveless, black Lycra

top with a vertical white stripe down each side. It looked pretty small, but the stretchy fabric would give it a snug fit over my flat chest. I accepted the top and held it up against the skirt.

"That would make a nice combo, I think. I'll go try these on."

Nicole smiled wickedly. "If you have your problem again, let me help. That has to be more fun than just waiting for it to go away."

I blushed deeply, but nodded. "I'll let you take care of it this time."

We made our way back to the fitting area. I claimed an empty room, Nicole took the one next to it. I spent a moment looking at myself in the mirror before I did anything else. As hard as I tried not to be vain, seeing myself always made me feel pretty.

I ran my hands down the front of my blouse, then started undoing the buttons. I did so slowly, watching intently as I did. My hips slowly swayed and gyrated while I undid my top. I wasn't just getting undressed, I was giving myself a striptease.

As I got more into the show the mirror was giving me, I tried to make it more of a dance. Soon, I pulled the top open to expose my flat chest and pink nipples. It was times like this that I envied Nicole's bust; I'd love to be able to flash myself with a pair of tits.

I folded my blouse and set it aside, then eased out of my skirt. I turned around and looked over my shoulder, watching my round butt slip free of the gray fabric. Purple panties clung to my bottom, tight fitting and slightly translucent. Once the skirt was off, I turned and thrust towards the mirror a few times. The bulge in the front of my panties was my only masculine feature. I felt myself starting to get a hard-on, so I quit dancing and instead reached for the new clothes.

I put the skirt on first. It fit well and looked marvelous. The fabric was thin enough that I could just barely see the outline of my purple underwear. Next I pulled the Lycra top on. It fit my contours perfectly and really did look good with the skirt. It was cut a little short though and showed off some belly. A few inches below the neckline, where my cleavage would be, was a heart-shaped hole.

Now dressed, I checked myself out in the mirror. It was as likeable a combination as I'd imagined. I did a few sexy poses, lusting after my own girly figure. I lifted the skirt just a little to give myself a flash of panty. I could feel my dick getting hard, but I didn't care anymore.

I pulled down the front of my panties a little to let my hardening cock free. My underwear was stretchy to an extent, but I was always afraid that getting fully hard in them too often would ruin them. I stared at it in the mirror—seven inches of thick stiffness, throbbing with need. My petite, girly figure made it look even bigger by comparison.

I stepped a little closer to the wall that separated the fitting rooms and spoke softly, "Nicole?"

"Yeah?"

"It's happening again."

"Unlock the door, I'm coming over."

I clicked the latch open. A couple of seconds later, Nicole came in wearing some of the clothes she'd picked out. Her torso was clad in a skin-tight, white minidress with a diagonal hem that stopped just above her knee on one side but high up her thigh on the other. It was white with red, blue, green, and yellow circles of varying sizes. The neckline was low-cut, showing off that fantastic cleavage. She also had on rainbow-striped thigh socks and shiny white boots that came about knee-high. The outfit itself was a little ridiculous, though I had to admit she looked pretty good in it.

My hot blonde ladyfriend stared at my erection with a smile. "You poor thing. Can't even look at yourself in the mirror without getting a stiffie, can you? You're too straight and too girly for your own good."

"Would you change me if you could?"

"Not a thing, darling. Not in a million years."

"I didn't bring any condoms, that kind of limits our options."

"That's okay, I'll let you stick it in my butt."

My eyes went wide. "Really?"

"Sure! Today feels like a good day to try something new. Just promise to be gentle."

"I promise, I'll be as gentle as a lamb."

Nicole smirked. "I've never been fucked by a lamb, sweetie, so I wouldn't know." We shared a laugh, then she continued. "Get comfy on your back; I need to get you ready with my mouth."

I pushed my clothes to one end of the bench and lied down. My stiff member jutted up into the air, throbbing madly. Nicole gave it a couple of soft strokes, then kissed the tip. She stepped away and pulled off her silky white panties, then climbed overtop of me. Her hands slid the hem of that silly looking skirt up, giving me an eyeful of her amazing pussy.

I gave Nicole's slit a few licks, then licked her ass instead. She clenched and shivered. "Ooh, dirty boy!"

"I have to get you ready too, don't I?"

Nicole wrapped her sexy lips around my tool and sucked. She drooled freely on my length, covering me in her saliva and using her lips to spread it. I swirled my tongue around her rosebud in slow circles until it relaxed a little. Then, I pressed my tongue up into her virgin pucker. I felt her moan more than I heard it.

After just a few minutes of suction, Nicole pulled her lovely mouth off of my cock. It strained, yearning for more of her touch, but she climbed off of me. The sexy blonde stood and leaned forward, pressing her hands to the mirror for support and waving her immaculate butt at me.

I got off of the bench as well and knelt behind her to give her ass a few more licks. Afterwards I stood and nudged her pucker with the tip of my cock. It was a mess of smeared lipstick and slobber, but it was definitely slick. I nudged her hole and felt her clench. After a few experimental pokes, she relaxed and I pushed the tip inside.

Nicole gasped and clenched, squeezing the head of my cock in her wondrous ass. I waited until she had relaxed again, then began to slowly inch my way inside her. Every time she clenched, I held still and waited for her to relax. It took some time, but my hips eventually pressed against her ass. My skirt lifted in the front, while hers lifted in the back; we stayed in that exact position for a few minutes.

"How do you feel?"

"Stretched, this is like being a virgin all over again."

"I won't make you cry this time, I promise."

Nicole smiled. "That's sweet, but I think I'll be okay. This actually isn't as bad as I imagined."

"Does that mean you're ready to continue?"

"Yes please!"

I drew back slowly, pulling my dick out of her ass a little at a time. I slid back in with equal slowness. A low groan passed from her lips for the entire duration of the inward push. I took her in slow, easy thrusts. Her groans slowly transitioned into quiet, wavering moans.

Nicole pressed her tush back to me a little more. "Faster, please."

I obeyed her request, moving my hips just a little faster. She squeaked adorably with every inward stroke now, but clenched tight while I pulled out each time. I gyrated in a steady rythm, watching my thickness disappear and reappear between her cheeks again and again.

Nicole leaned forward more, pressing her cheek to the mirror. One of her hands moved to massage her tit through the white dress while the other snuck between her legs. She was panting, and her breath fogged up the mirror. I gave her a firm swat on the ass and started to take her harder.

My hips slapped Nicole's ass audibly. It was becoming harder and harder to keep my voice down, my own girly moans soon joined hers. She soon came with a cry of bliss. Her butt clenched up tight and I had to thrust harder to keep up the same pace.

"Not so hard, you're tearing me apart!"

"Sorry." I eased up considerably. "Better?"

"Much, thank you."

I leaned forward and kissed Nicole on the cheek. My hand brushed hers away from her tit, and I massaged both of her breasts at once. She moved her free hand down to her crotch as well, fingering herself with one and teasing her clit with the other. I could feel myself getting close already, but tried to hold back. When Nicole came again, I let it go as well. I thrust deep into her ass and let out a shrill moan. My member throbbed hard and shot a big load of my sticky spunk deep in her tight ass. I squeezed her breasts and ground my hips against her butt.

We both just stood there, panting. After about five minutes, Nicole spoke. "That was better than I expected. We'll have to experiment some more later."

"How about right now?"

I pulled back an inch and gave her a

short, hard thrust. She moaned and pressed her rump back to me. I released her tits and moved one hand to her hip. The other hand grabbed a handful of her hair and pulled playfully. I fucked her ass hard and fast, making her scream.

"You little son of a bitch!"

"Want me to stop?"

"No, it's hurting in a good way now. Your cum isn't a half bad lubricant!"

I slapped her ass again, hard enough to leave a mark this time. My thrusts pulled cum out of her and made it dribble down her thighs and soak into her thigh socks. My balls slapped her pussy hard every time I sheathed my sword in her glorious bottom.

My humping sped up even more. Nicole screamed and squealed, soon coming to a third climax. I was positively destroying her ass, and she was loving it. I'd never been this rough with her before, but I found myself enjoying the brutality.

I didn't last much longer like that. A climax crept up on me without warning, and I couldn't hold back at the pace I was going. I moaned again, and continued pounding her throughout my orgasm. Another load of semen burst into Nicole's tush, spilling out of her stretched hole with every thrust. My pounding hips smeared cum all over both of us and splashed it over her cheeks.

Once I came down from my peak, I held myself inside Nicole for a few seconds. Reluctantly, I pulled completely out of her and sat on the bench. My stiff but spent cock softened in the cool air. Once it had fully returned to its dormant state, I tucked it into my panties.

Nicole continued to lean on the mirror for a while, panting heavily. Once she'd recovered, she straightened her skirt and put her panties back on. She sat on the bench next to me with a slight wince and kissed my lips.

"That was fun, but next time we do it that rough we need to use real lube."

"Agreed, my cock is on fire."

Nicole laughed. "You're complaining? I'm surprised I'm not bleeding! How'd you know I like rough sex?"

"I didn't, I wanted to see if you do or not."

"Well, I guess trial and error works. You could have asked, though."

"Where's the fun in that?"

We shared a laugh, then she spoke again. "You know, ethically I think we have to buy these clothes now."

I nodded. "It's just common courtesy. I'd hate to take something with cum stains off the rack."

Nicole kissed me again, then stood. She made her way back to the other dressing room, walking slightly funny. We both changed into our original outfits, then took our purchases to the counter. Some of the other customers looked at us and giggled. The store clerk gave us the dirtiest of looks while ringing up our purchases. The look on her face when she accidentally touched a gooey spot made the mild embarrassment totally worth it.

7 GIRLIER
GIRLY PART 2

I stole glances at the beautiful blonde next to me. She made it look so easy. Her breasts had always been nicely sized, but I'd only recently gotten augmentation surgery for myself. The new additions to my formerly flat chest threw off my center of gravity. I was being made to relearn the concept of balance.

Every step felt awkward. The bouncing sensation, in particular, was a constant distraction. I could see Nicole looking at me too, smiling. The implants were her idea. She said I needed them so my shirts would fit better. That was true, in a way. It was much easier to find a fitting top now. However, she hadn't stopped smiling since I agreed to get the surgery. Something about her demeanor told me she was more interested in my bust enhancement than she let on. My bruises and stitches healed quickly. I wasn't down for recovery long at all. My boobs were still quite tender, though. One morning, Nicole suggested we take a walk together so that I can show them off. I wasn't entirely thrilled with the idea, but I needed the fresh air.

Nicole was wearing a shiny, bright green bikini top that left her cleavage exposed for the whole world to see. Her bottom was poured into a pair of tight cutoff shorts. They barely concealed more than her underwear would have, if she was even wearing underwear. On her feet were a pair of black leather sandals, leaving her toes exposed. Her nails were painted different colors. Each foot formed a rainbow, with the exception of indigo and violet.

The outfit I had chosen was quite a bit more sensible. A deep brown tank top hugged my bosom. It showed off the goods without being too revealing. The color also went nicely with my mahogany hair. I also had on a short, forest green skirt and a pair of brown sneakers. I'd been on an earthy colors kick lately, breaking my usual devotion to monochromatic ensembles. Our walk mostly passed without incident. I caught a few guys staring and had to smirk—if only they knew they weren't ogling a woman. Nicole got the majority of the attention, though. It wasn't just her blonde hair or her stunning body, I had to attribute part of it to attitude. She wanted to be noticed, and guys were all too happy to oblige.

Lost in my thoughts, I didn't notice Nicole

sneaking behind me. In a single, swift, calculated motion, she lifted my top and bared my bosoms to everyone nearby. I squealed and tried to right my top, but she wouldn't let me.

"Nicole, stop it! What is the matter with you?"

"You said you didn't mind showing them off!"

"I thought that's what the tank top was for?"

"It doesn't count if they can't see your nipples, silly!"

To my great relief, she released my top and allowed me to pull it back down. My face felt hot. I was blushing harder than ever before. Men had stopped mid-step, mostly joggers and dog walkers. They stared at me, smiling.When their attention shifted to the blonde nutcase on my left, I looked at her as well. Her own perky breasts were now on display. The bikini top had offered little resistance in being moved aside. I stared, feeling a peculiar mix of embarrassment and arousal.

"You have problems."

"Stop being such a prude, dear!"

"You're going to get us arrested!"

"Oh, pish posh apple sauce. Come on, Jamie, get your girls out! Let's show off together, as a couple."

I stared at the ground. After a moment, I hesitantly lifted my top. My cheeks burned. They may not have been naturally mine, but I still felt weird showing them to strangers. I actively avoided looking at the crowd. My eyes remained glued to the ground while they gawked at my faux mammaries. Nicole stepped closer to me and nudged my arm with an elbow.

"Let's give these guys a real show."

"What do you mean? Going all Girls Gone Wild at the dog park isn't enough?"

"No. Squish your tits against mine and kiss me."

I was dumbfounded by the request, but I obeyed. Turning to face my lover, I embraced her and pressed in close. My bare breasts squished against hers. I pressed my lips to hers and slipped her some tongue, then got some tongue in return. I could hear our audience cheer, but I remained focused on kissing Nicole.

My hands remained at her lower back, but I could feel her naughty hands roaming all over my body. She caressed and groped up and down my back. Every touch brought a new wave of embarrassment. However, I could feel my own exhibitionist side awakening. My cock grew hard within my soft cotton panties. Nicole undoubtedly noticed my stiffening member while grinding her crotch against mine.

Suddenly, Nicole lifted the back of my skirt. I broke the kiss with a gasp and reached back to lower it. It occurred to me that preventing them from seeing my panties was an odd distinction to make, considering they'd already seen my bare chest. While I was distracted righting my skirt, Nicole had dug a condom out of her pocket and pressed it against my chest.

"Suit up."

"What? Right here?"

"We're going to get nasty on that bench."

"You and your exhibitionism..."

"Oh don't even start, you know you've got a splash of it, too."

"As a fantasy! Doing it in a fitting room or public restroom or even the back seat of your car is fine, but in front of a crowd at the park is too much! I don't want all of these people to see my thing!"

"Oh relax, you're a big guy. Nobody is going to think otherwise."

"That's not my point."Nicole brazenly reached under my skirt and grabbed my growing erection.

"Look at how stiff you are! You can't tell me you don't need this taken care of."

I sighed. "Fine. How do you want me?"

"Just sit down and make yourself comfortable, let me do all of the work."

I sat on the bench and tried to relax. Nicole sat next to me and immediately moved the front of my skirt out of her way. Next, she pulled down the front of my panties to expose my throbbing shaft. The crowd fell deathly silent. I could just barely hear some of the men whispering to each other. My blush grew deeper. I wondered how it must feel for them to discover that the hot brunette they were ogling was actually a guy.

Nicole didn't let me feel the breeze on my cock for very long. Her hot mouth soon engulfed my sensitive tool. She took the whole thing easily. Her lips and tongue teased me exquisitely. My penis strained, almost as if it were trying to jump off of my groin.

Nicole slid her mouth off of my length, then nibbled up the side of it. The feel of her teeth on my rod made me squirm. She looked up at me with a devilish expression and lightly chewed on my glans—not hard enough to hurt, but enough to keep me wiggling. She teased the sensitive head first with her incisors, then with her molars.

Once she was through chewing on my dick, Nicole sat up and tore open the condom wrapper. She rolled the latex sleeve onto my twitching erection, then stroked me to smooth out all of the bubbles. Satisfied that the condom was on thoroughly, she stood up. Nicole shed her cutoffs, and the crowd of men cheered to see that she lacked a penis. Now bottomless, the lovely blonde straddled me.

Only a thin layer of latex separated my raging erection from her moist, pink slit. She ground her crotch against mine for a few minutes, teasing us both. Once she was done messing with me, she lowered herself onto my prick. The tip parted her folds. I watched my length slowly disappear into her.

Nicole took her time impaling herself. My rod throbbed powerfully within her tight embrace. Her pussy flexed in response, massaging my rigid pillar of flesh. She ever so slowly slid lower. Time stood still, there was nothing left of the world but the two of us and the love we shared.

Finally, our crotches met. I let out a breath I didn't know I was holding. My latex-clad cock was fully within her now. She held her position for a few seconds so that we could savor each other's bodies. Then, she kissed me and began to lift up.

My soul mate rode me in slow, deep strokes. Her movements were very deliberate. It was only when her nipples brushed mine that I realized we both still had our tits out. Momentarily brought back to reality, I looked beyond Nicole. Our onlookers had grown in number. Many of them now had their cell phones out, recording us.

Nicole sensed my distraction and began moving faster. I threw my head back with a moan. My hands latched onto her immaculate butt and squeezed. For a while, I didn't care that we were being watched. Her muff was making a very convincing case in favor of exhibitionism.

My own hips began moving in time with hers. I couldn't stop if I wanted to. My hard pole disappeared into her glistening mound again and again. I concentrated and tuned out the chatter of the pepping toms. All I wanted to hear was my lover breathing.I lowered my head and buried my face between her soft tits. She wrapped her arms around me and hugged me into her bosom. Those amazing hips of hers rolled even faster, and I sped up to match. I could feel a familiar tingle, and I knew I wouldn't last much longer.

Nicole was the first to cum. She dropped

firmly onto my lap and cried out. The musical sound of her climax pushed me over the edge. I bucked up into her and let out a moan that was muffled by her amazing tits. My cock trembled within her and filled the tip of the condom.

I withdrew my face from Nicole's breasts and let my head hang back. I could barely hear our collective panting over the cheers and laughter of those around us. My cheeks burned brightly, but I knew it was too late to do anything now. They'd already seen it all, some had even recorded it. Our playtime was probably going to show up online, somewhere.

My train of thought was derailed by a kiss. I closed my eyes and allowed myself to get lost in the smooch. She slipped me some tongue, and I gave her mine. For a little while, we held one another and exchanged moans.

My penis remained hard as a rock inside Nicole. After a few moments of kissing, she took her angelic lips away and lifted herself off of me. She turned around and replanted herself in my lap. I moaned softly and grasped her hips. She placed her hands on my thighs and gently lowered herself onto my rigid pole again.

Once she got settled in, Nicole began to bounce swiftly. Her bare ass slapped my pelvis audibly. I couldn't see anything beyond the golden hair in front of my face, but I just knew her tits were bouncing around for everyone to see.

Nicole leaned forward and began to ride

me even harder. I threw my head back and moaned for her, sounding just like a girl. She rewarded my effeminate vocalization with a tight clench. After a few good slams, she leaned back against me and held still. I shifted forward slightly, grabbed her by the thighs, and began to thrust up into her as quickly as my position allowed.

I gnashed my teeth and tried to make it last. In just minutes, I lost control and buried myself deep. With a long moan, I came for the second time that day. My cock pulsed and added to the mess already in the condom, making it feel very squishy inside. Nicole reached down to touch herself and soon had a climax of her own. The clenching on my oversensitive penis made me squirm.

We rested in that position for a little while. I rubbed her sides and played with her tits while she caressed my thighs and fondled my balls. Neither of us cared that people were taking pictures. What we'd just shared was totally worth it.When the two of us had caught our breath, Nicole stood up. She turned and knelt, then pulled the condom off of my softening tool. Her lips touched my tip in a tender kiss, then she reached for her shorts. She got dressed, then we both righted our tops and shared another kiss. Nicole discarded the filled condom into a nearby trash can without breaking lip-lock.

The rest of the walk passed in peace. We held hands the whole way, neither one of us was able to stop smiling. We continued to get looks from passersby, but that was normal. We shared a long shower when we got home and then took a nap together.

In time, I got used to having breasts. It was a big adjustment, but something I learned to enjoy. My body was forever changed, but I was already very girly before. The implants just made me girlier. Of course, it had become almost impossible for me to use a mirror without getting hard. Luckily, Nicole was always nearby to take care of me.

8 NEED

I sighed and counted the cracks in the ceiling. Scott could tell I was bored and adjusted his hips to thrust into me at a different angle. He was a nice enough guy, sure, and I could feel the sensations from what he was doing. But I just couldn't get turned on for him. No matter what he did, it never thrilled me. He could provide a pleasant tingle, but that wasn't enough to get me off.

He had tried so many different things to please me, despite my telling him not to worry about it. I could get myself off well enough; I didn't need him to do it for me. I didn't mind having sex with him. That is what lovers do, after all. It didn't hurt me any to keep him satisfied. The effort he put into trying to make it good for me too was a little heart-breaking, though. Seeing my disinterest fuel his feelings of inferiority made me feel like a cruel bitch, but I couldn't help it. Faking it would be as bad as lying, and I considered that even more cruel.

I knew what would work in the bedroom, but I could never tell him. I really do love the poor guy. Keeping such a big secret from him hurt, but I was so afraid it would make things worse if I told him. My bright green eyes drifted around the room, mapping out the ceiling while he had his fun. I did this every night, it helped pass the time.

I let my mind wander enough that I almost forgot I was being fucked. Scott's sudden grunt startled me, I actually jumped a little. Brought back to reality, I could feel his tool throbbing inside me. He ground his hips against mine for a few seconds, then pulled out. He removed the condom from his average prick and tossed it into the bedside trashcan.

"Are you all right? You seem more distracted than usual."

"I'm fine, I'm just really tired."

"Did you feel anything this time?"

"I felt it, yeah. I always do."

"Just tell me what I'm doing wrong."

"You aren't doing anything wrong."

"Come on Julia, help me out here. I just want to make you feel good."

"It's not you, it's me."

"That's a little cliché, isn't it?"

"Yes, but true. As long as you got off, that's the important thing."

"Don't say that, your pleasure is

important too. I always feel so selfish in bed."

"Selfish? Not at all honey, you try so hard to please me. I just don't think that you can."

"So that's it? Nothing I can do will get you off?"

"Don't worry about it, I've got working hands. I can get myself off."

"Yeah, me too. But sex is supposed to be mutual, I want it to be as good for you as it is for me."

"Scott, sweetie, some things just require a woman's touch."

He grinned. "Oh, I see. I think I understand, now."

I blushed deeply, scared and embarrassed that I might have just outed myself. "I didn't mean it like that! Stop smiling that way, I'm not talking about that at all!" I rolled onto my side and pulled the bed sheet over my head. "Just go to sleep, pervert!"

Scott lay down beside me and put an arm around me. "Love you, Julia."

I lowered the sheet and pressed back to him. "Love you too, Scotty."

Though he was asleep in minutes, I stared at the wall all night. My mind raced. I had very nearly outed myself to him entirely by accident. I hoped he was joking, and that he would disregard the entire conversation. He seemed okay with the idea, but I was still terrified by the thought of him knowing. The stress had my belly cramping all throughout the night.

I must have eventually drifted off, because I was asleep enough for the alarm to wake me. I turned it off, then sat up and stretched. Scott wasn't in the bed anymore. I showered, got dressed, and left for work. He was nowhere in the house. I could have sworn he had the day off, but I didn't think anything of it.

Having a uniform that consisted of only a vest, I was free to wear pretty much whatever I wanted. A short tan skirt and a sleeveless gray top made for a nice outfit in the warm weather. My employer's dress code prohibited open-toed shoes though, which was a pity. I felt like my white sneakers took away from the outfit a little.

My shift at work was entirely uneventful, the same routine as almost every other day. I didn't mind. I actually enjoy my job. It was the sort of rut I didn't mind falling into. Things didn't get interesting until after work.

I was walking home when I noticed a beautiful, dark-haired woman. She wore a pair of black leather boots, knee-high with buckles all the way up. Black leather pants clung to her shapely legs like a second skin. Her upper body was clad in a black leather vest, only half-zipped to make it clear that she wore nothing underneath.

The woman in black leather walked towards me, closing the distance fast. I was too distracted by her looks to even notice until she was right in front of me. Startled, I took a step back. Her lips curled into a smile, and the coating of cherry-red lipstick held my attention.

"You're Julia, aren't you? You're even sexier than I expected."

I recoiled. "Hold on. Who are you? How do you know my name? Why would you be expecting anything?"

"That's not important right now. You may call me mistress, and all will be revealed soon enough. Come, I'm taking you home with me."

"Excuse me? You're awfully forward! For your information, I have a boyfriend. And furthermore, I don't even know you!"

"You know me as well as you need to know me, and I know you as well as I need to know you. I can do things to you that your boyfriend couldn't even dream of."

"But I'm not..."

Before I could breathe another word, she grabbed my arms and kissed me fiercely. My eyes went wide, but I couldn't find the strength to pull away. Her tongue wormed into my mouth and undulated in a display of oral talent. I'd be lying if I said it didn't turn me on a little.

As hard as I tried to believe this was wrong, it felt right. A few seconds into the intense kiss, I relaxed. I had never kissed another woman before, but being tongued by this stranger erased all doubts of lesbianism from my mind. With my token resistance tamed, my mistress moved her hands to grope me. Her hands cupped and squeezed my breasts through my shirt. My nipples grew hard for her and were rewarded with teasing pinches. I was being felt up in public by someone I'd never met before. Every part of me screamed that I should make her stop. And yet, there was just something about her that made me feel meek and submissive.

I finally broke out of the powerful kiss when my mistress's touch snuck lower. That naughty hand disappeared beneath my skirt to stroke me through my panties. I gasped sharply at the initial touch, then wiggled.

"In public? Are you crazy? People will see us!"

"Relax, no one is going to care."

Though still worried, I did relax. I believed her because I wanted to believe her. She had some sort of hold on me. I couldn't tell whether it was a power she possessed, or just my own repressed desire working against me. Either way, exercising good judgment was the furthest thing from my mind.

My mistress slipped her hand inside my panties to stroke my pussy directly, eliciting a soft cry from me. I was already sopping wet for her. She only provided a teasing caress, though. No amount of wishing got her to slip a finger inside.

Any normal woman would have slapped her for being so brazen, but I couldn't even muster the willpower to ask her to stop. I knew this was a bad idea, but I also needed it on so many levels. I craved a woman's touch, in body and soul. I could deny my true desires no longer.

I lost track of time. Seconds felt like hours, minutes felt like weeks. My mistress kept up the same slow, torturous teasing. I humped her hand, hoping for more, but she wouldn't take it to the next level. Finally, I'd had enough and cried out.

"Finish me!"

"I won't if that's how you're going to ask. I want you to beg for it."

"Please, make me cum!"

"You are to refer to me as 'mistress' when you make a request."

"Please mistress, make me cum! I need it!"

"Good girl."

I blushed, partly in frustration and partly in embarrassment. The odd comment was swiftly pushed from my mind when two of her slender fingers slid into my delicate pink. I clenched and let out a quiet whimper. My voice rose into an enthusiastic moan when her fantastic touch migrated to my g-spot.

Mistress worked my favorite place like a pro. My legs felt like jelly, I had to hold her shoulders to keep myself from falling to the ground. My whole body quaked with need, and she did not disappoint.

When a much-needed climax finally washed over me, I couldn't stay quiet for any amount of effort. A scream of ecstasy burst from my lungs, making our activity abundantly clear to everyone in earshot. I didn't care if anyone heard. I was completely focused on the beautiful, raven-haired woman and what she was doing to me.

Mistress's talented fingers continued to massage my pussy for a few more seconds. When she pulled her digits free, I felt a sudden sensation of loss. She brought a very wet hand up to stroke my cheek. The breeze made me keenly aware of the moisture she was smearing on my face.

"That was just a preview, my dear. Come with me and I shall treat you to erotic delights beyond your wildest dreams."

"I will do anything you say, mistress."

I couldn't believe those words had come out of my mouth. With a smile, she took my hand and led me away from the familiar route I walked each day. Temporarily broken from her spell, I noticed just how many people had been watching. The revelation was simultaneously humiliating and arousing.

My mistress took me down an alley and into a parking lot. She stopped near a black Cadillac and dug a keychain from one of the pockets on her vest. With the tap of a button on her key fob, the doors unlocked. She opened the passenger-side door and gestured for me to get in. I did so immediately. Just a moment later, the driver-side door opened and a vision in black leather joined me in the luxury sedan. She slipped the key in the ignition and turned, bringing the engine to life. The drive passed in silence, giving me some time to think. Time not well spent. My mind was a muddled mess, I couldn't tell up from down anymore. As the drive dragged on and on though, I did realize one thing. Our meeting was no accident. Once it became clear that she lived in the far end of town, the absurdity of the situation really set in.

This woman knew when I got off work, what path I walked to get home, what I look like, and even my name. She was also obviously waiting for me. This whole thing had to have been planned, and I couldn't fathom why. The more I thought about it, the creepier it all seemed. I wondered briefly if she was a stalker, but the thought vanished from my mind when the car's engine shut off.

We were parked in front of a nice-looking, suburban house. I'd never been to this part of town, and I doubted my ability to find my way home on my own. My mistress exited the car. I hesitated briefly, then got out as well. I was led by the hand up a concrete walkway. Behind me, I could hear the Cadillac's car alarm beep twice. My legs suddenly felt very heavy as we approached the front door to her house. I didn't know what sorts of things she intended to do to me in here. I was afraid to find out. Nevertheless, I couldn't bring myself to escape her hold.

The inside of the house was surprisingly ordinary. I expected a fetish dungeon, but my mistress's home was nothing of the sort. Her house was decorated in nicer, more expensive versions of the same sort of furniture Scott and I owned. Everything was posh and gorgeous.

My mistress led me down a hall, to her

bedchamber. This room actually was a fetish dungeon. Only a skylight illuminated the room. It lit up the center but kept the edges and corners dark. There were lamps, but none of them were on. I could also see a sex swing, bondage gear, a rack of whips in varying sizes and shapes, and a box overflowing with dildos.

Before I could more thoroughly examine my surroundings, mistress took me in another forceful kiss. I moaned into her mouth and suckled her tongue. While tongue-fucking me in the mouth, she unzipped and removed her vest. Reluctantly, I broke the kiss and pulled off my top. I shed my bra, skirt, panties, sneakers, and socks next. Though my mistress had only her pants and boots left to remove, peeling out of her leather pants took a while.

Once we were both fully nude, mistress shoved me onto the bed. She soon joined me, and straddled my face. Her moist pussy slid across my lips, and I accepted her nonverbal request without hesitation. My tongue slid between her folds and began to wiggle as quickly as I could move it. I hoped my enthusiasm could make up for my lack of experience. Her moans told me I was doing something right. I tried to put my tongue in different places and wiggle in different patterns, listening intently so I could know what pleased her the most.

Her sweet flavor flowed over my tongue, a never-ending dribble of ambrosia from her fountain of desire. Her taste and scent were intoxicating I couldn't get enough of her. I gave no thought to my own pleasure; both of my hands were busy kneading mistress's immaculate bottom.

I would have been content to eat mistress's pussy forever. It wasn't meant to last, though. Sooner than I'd hoped, she came. Her fluids gushed over my face, thicker and more flavorful than before. I drank as much of her orgasmic fluid as she could give. I was actually a little sad when she sat up, taking the wonderful treat away from me.

Mistress made her way to the end of the bed. She reached into her toy box and felt around for a few minutes. Then, she pulled out an 18-inch horse dildo attached to a leather harness. I gawked at the silicone monument to sex. I was simultaneously terrified of what she might intend to do with it, and disgusted with myself for recognizing the shape.

"Whoa! Where do you think that's going?"

"Wherever I want it to. I am your mistress, and you will obey me."

I felt torn inside. My brain told me to run away, my gut told me to punch this bitch for her attitude, and my heart told me to give in and play her games. After some uncomfortable squirming, I nodded meekly.

"Yes, mistress."

"Good girl. Now, get on all fours. Before I breed my obedient little mare, she must first look the part." I rolled over and sat up on my hands and knees. My mistress put a bit in my mouth, then shoved a horse tail butt plug up my ass. I groaned, muffled by the bit, and clenched around the thick plug. It was uncomfortably wide in my virginal ass, but I endured for mistress. Next, she placed a heavy but comfortable leather saddle on my back and adjusted the straps until it held me snugly.

This was becoming stranger by the minute. After mistress strapped on the horse-cock dildo, she inserted a second horse tail plug into her own ass. She slapped my face with the thick toy, then moved behind me; I felt the girth slide between my legs, grinding against my pussy. It was easily as thick as my wrist, and the thought of taking it made me squirm.   "My dirty little mare is in heat, isn't she? Beg for your stallion to breed you, mare! Let me hear you whinny."

I did my best imitation of a horse, muffled by the bit in my mouth. My vocalizations swiftly changed to a yelp of surprise when mistress used her horse phallus to spank me.

"Louder! Make me believe you really need it!"

I tossed my head back and tried again, this time as loud as I could manage without removing the bit. I whinnied again and again, making a fool of myself at my mistress's command. As frightening as the fake horse tool was, I found myself genuinely craving it. I was eager to cater to her every whim, even if it meant acting like a horse and getting screwed with what was essentially a rubber arm.

My needful whinnies had apparently

grown more convincing. Mistress finally rewarded my efforts with the tip of her dildo. I felt the thickness nudge my glistening petals apart, then oh so slowly sink into my tight muff. The silicone was soft and squished down a bit on the way in. It stretched my pussy comfortably, and expanded as I loosened up.

Mistress probed deeper and deeper with her stallion toy. I'd never had anything so long and thick inside me. I felt like a virgin all over again. I let out a sharp grunt when the tip of the toy nudged my cervix. Mistress tapped my innermost limit a few more times, just to see me squirm.

Once she was done watching me writhe, mistress slowly pulled out. She hesitated with only the tip inside, then roughly buried the toy again. I screamed around the bit and clenched tight. Mistress grabbed the reigns in one and hand and slapped my ass with the other. She took me hard and fast, with little regard for my comfort.

To my amusement, mistress made some horse sounds of her own. She wasn't much better at them than I. Her goofy sounding neighs and nickers made me grateful to have my voice muffled. I'd hate to be caught laughing at her. Mistress played the part of a stallion well. She crammed that big cock into me like she was trying to break me. The experience was a little painful, quite uncomfortable, and extremely arousing.

I became very wet for my mistress. My slick muff sauce made each coming thrust easier. Soon, I could hear the sound of the toy sliding in and out of me over the awkward noises mistress was making. Once I started getting used to the silicone horse cock, I tried to make some horse noises as well. It wasn't easy with the bit in my mouth. I also wasn't entirely sure what sort of noises horses made, aside from a whinny. I tried to imitate mistress, and found it to be harder than she made it seem.

The more I relaxed, the faster mistress humped. She kept up with me perfectly, ensuring I constantly rode the line between bliss and discomfort. It wasn't long before my body began to shake. I wouldn't be able to take much more of this. Another firm slap to my upturned derrière only brought me closer.

"Is the slutty little mare going to cum for her stallion?"

"Mmmmph!"

"Cum for me, cum for your mistress! Let me hear you neigh!"

I needed no further bidding. I arched my back and whinnied as loud as I could. My pussy clenched erratically around the fat toy. Mistress sped up her humping even more and whinnied as well. She ground the head of the horse cock against my cervix, making me writhe under her.

A grunt from the corner of the room caught my attention. I could just vaguely see a figure in the darkness, but I couldn't make out who it was. Mistress dismounted me and removed the bit from my mouth, then turned on the lights.

"Scott?! What are you doing here?"

"He set this whole thing up," said mistress. "He thinks you're a closet lesbian, so he hired me to show you a good time."

Scott smiled warmly and put his dick away. "I didn't think things would get this weird, but it was a great show anyway."

"Scott, why would you do something like this?"

"What do you mean? Didn't you have fun?"

"I did, but you didn't have to do this for me."

"I hate having fun in bed while you just lie there, bored. It's just not fair to you. I paid for Mistress Isabella's services to follow up on a hunch of mine. I wanted to see if you're really into women."

"I guess this means I am. I'm sorry, Scott."

"Don't be, I'm not at all upset. I just don't know where to go from here."

I stood up from the bed, then removed the saddle and butt plug. Scott stood up as well, and I hugged him tightly. He shamelessly caressed my nude body, taking advantage of the situation to touch my everything. And in front of mistress too, the nerve of that man!

"Scott, I'm in love with you. I just can't get excited about sleeping with a man, nothing personal."

"I love you too, Julia. I hope this doesn't

mean we have to breakup?"

"No, I have a better idea. We find another woman. Someone bisexual, someone we can both have fun with. Someone who can have her fun with either of us."

"I like the way you think! If we find a third, then nothing else will have to change."

We both glanced over at Mistress Isabella, who was enjoying a post-coital cigarette on the bed. When she noticed the attention, she sat up straight. "Whoa, don't look at me! I'm only in this for the money; you two will have to find someone else for your long-term three-way."

9 DEMON SEED

Aclear, crisp bing-bong echoed through the halls of the small suburban home. Seconds later, the sound repeated itself. I hurried to the door, my curly blond locks bouncing with each step. I looked through the peephole and saw a pale man with a dark goatee. He wore an all-red, three-piece suit and matching fedora. I quickly unlocked the door and pulled it open.

"Hello, sir! Please, come in! What brings you by today?"

The man politely removed his hat, freeing a short mane of shiny black hair and revealing a small pair of horns on his forehead. He entered the house, bringing an unearthly chill in his wake. I shivered and shut the door, only to find that the cold wasn't coming from outside.

"I just came by to check up on you and

your family, Melissa. How is little Catherine doing? Feeling better, I hope?"

"Yes, she is! She's made a full recovery, in fact. It's some kind of miracle! Thank you so much, sir."

The devil smiled. "That is wonderful. It pains me to see a child fall ill; I am so glad that I could help. However, I am sure you remember that I requested some...compensation."

I frowned. "I do, Mr. Lucifer. Our next child will be yours, just as you asked."

"Please, Lucifer will do, dear. You need not be so formal with me. Now that your daughter has recovered, I have come to collect my end of the bargain."

"I don't understand. Collect how? My husband and I haven't had another child yet."

Lucifer laughed. "I think you misunderstood the terms of our deal, Melissa. Your next child will be mine, as in my own flesh and blood. I have come to father that child."

A deep blush colored my cheeks. "Oh, dear. I thought you meant our next child's soul or something. It was a hard thing to agree to, but this...."

"I do hope you aren't thinking of backing out of our agreement, dear."

"Well, no. I...I'd never betray you, Satan. You saved Catherine's life when no one else could do a thing. There are no traces of cancer in any part of her body. Our doctor even used the word 'miracle' to describe her recovery. To know my little girl is safe and healthy...that's worth anything."

"So, what's the problem?"

"I'm married! I would be betraying my husband if we were to do what you're asking. I need to talk to him about this. We misunderstood your terms. That's our fault, I'm sure. We got so excited we didn't ask many questions. But I need to discuss this. It's kind of a big thing to ask of a mortal."

"It's fine, sweetie." I whirled around to see my husband standing in the doorway.

"Trevor, my good man! How are you today, sir?"

"Doing great, Lucifer. Catherine is back to laughing and playing. It's as if nothing ever happened. To see her acting like a little kid again warms my heart. We are indebted to you, sir."

"Honey, we need to talk. I think you might not fully understand what we've agreed to."

"I heard him explain it to you. It's fine. I said I'd give anything to see Catherine recover, and I meant it. I have no objections to you sleeping with the devil."

Lucifer smiled. "Well then, Melissa. Shall we retire to somewhere more comfortable?"

I blushed and nodded. "Yes, Sir Lucifer."

I took the devil's hand and led him upstairs to the master bedroom. He shut the door behind him and began undressing. Blushing deeply, I began to get nude as well.

His physique was stunning; he had just the perfect level of musculature. By the look in his eyes, I could tell he appreciated my body as well.

Unable to shake the feeling of nervousness, I crawled into bed. The devil did not follow. He instead remained standing, watching me. I posed for him, trying to look sexy. He smiled, satisfied with my effort.

"I hope you don't mind, dear, but I am more comfortable doing this in my true form."

"Your true form?"

"This human body is just a facade. It's actually a rather uncomfortable disguise."

Lucifer's skin began to darken, going from his pale Caucasian skin tone to rich crimson in seconds. He grew taller until he was at least eight feet in height. His horns also grew, becoming very long and curled like those of a ram. Thick black fur grew all over his body. His feet warped into hooves, and his legs became very strong and sturdy looking. Even his face was hidden beneath his fur. I could only see his eyes, which glowed like hot coals.

"Ah, that's better." His voice had changed as well. It was a distorted, inhuman sound that filled me with dread.

The devil crawled onto bed with me. I instinctively backed away from his bestial figure. I felt something brush my thigh and looked down to see his semi-erect penis. As large as it was at half-mast, I doubted my ability to handle him fully erect.

My attempted retreat was halted by the bed's headboard. The devil gripped my thighs and stuck his head between my legs. I felt his long serpentine tongue slither into my pussy. It was thick, hot, and incredibly flexible. The feel of it undulating through my love canal had me trembling. My pussy quickly grew wet for him.

The delightful teasing ended after only a few minutes. He sat up on his knees, letting me see his erection. The shiny red flesh had grown fully engorged while he licked me. It was human enough in shape, but the size and color made it look grotesque. He was easily at full twelve inches long and just a bit thicker than my wrist.

For a while, I just stared in disbelief. I watched it pulsate and saw his precum drool from the bulbous tip. I had never taken anything so large inside me. However, as a mother, I knew my body was capable of stretching to accommodate him.

Whether or not I was capable of enjoying the experience was another question entirely.

"Are you ready?"

"As ready as I'll ever be. Just go easy on me, okay?"

"Of course, my dear. I wouldn't want to injure such a fine and delicate creature."

Satan kissed me on the lips, worming his slimy tongue into my mouth. I accepted the smooch and kissed back. I felt his hands roaming over my body; he was cold to the touch. He positioned me the way he wanted and then touched the end of his intimidating prick against my slick petals. The flesh of his penis was very hot, like his tongue. It seemed unaffected by the aura of chilly air that otherwise surrounded him.

Lucifer's rod parted my petals and eased inside. I groaned softly, feeling myself stretch wide for him. His precum was very slippery and eased the way for his mighty girth. True to his word, the devil was very gentle. His forward advance was very slow and easy.

I felt him slip further and further into me. So thick, so incredibly warm! Tingles surged through my lower body. I whimpered when he went deeper than I liked, and he took the hint. The devil drew back until only the head remained inside, then in as far as I was comfortable taking him. His powerful hips rolled slowly and steadily, giving me the most unbelievable dicking of my life.

My pussy was unbelievably wet. I was more turned on than I'd ever been in spite of, or perhaps because of, his girth. The devil's mighty cock plunged into me again and again, eliciting a lewd slurp from my moist snatch every time. I ran my fingers through his cold fur and clung to him tightly.

In no time, I came. My pussy squeezed him tightly while my body convulsed beneath his. My fluids squirted freely into his dark fur. He held himself still all throughout my climax, allowing me to wriggle and clench uninterrupted. He waited until my involuntary squirming ended before he resumed humping.

His thrusts were deeper now but just as slow as ever. It was a little uncomfortable to have him sliding so far in, but I didn't mind. He was a very gentle and generous lover. His tender behavior utterly defied his intimidating appearance.

My hips swiveled and bucked beyond my ability to control them. Any reservations my mind had to being impregnated by another man were overturned by my body. The first orgasm had weakened my defenses. The next came more quickly. Just as the last time, the devil halted his motions while I came, and resumed when I was done.

"Faster!"

Satan heeded my request. His hips began to buck more swiftly. I tugged at his long fur and screamed, wracked with unbelievable pleasure. Mixed fluids splashed hotly onto my thighs. His glistening pole was bathed in my nectar even as it summoned more.

"Faster!"

Lucifer picked up the pace. He was churning me like butter. I screamed and came again. This time, he continued to thrust all through my climax. Soon after, I experienced a fourth peak. Then, a fifth. They were getting closer together and exponentially more intense. By the time the sixth hit, I felt like I was going to pass out.

When the devil began to tense up and fell out of rhythm, I knew he was getting close.

Prince of Darkness or not, he was still a man and could be read like a book. I clenched tighter for him and wrapped my legs around his hulking frame. I could feel myself riding the edge of a seventh orgasm, and I did my best to hold it back.

"Cum with me, Satan!"

The devil humped even faster. His raw bestial strength jarred my petite body. Just as I felt I couldn't hold it in any longer, he reached his peak. Satan wedged the tip of his enormous dick against my cervix, then threw his head back and let out an inhuman roar. My voice mingled with his, a climactic scream. I could feel his burning hot seed surge into my body. Every spurt of thick, hot syrup made me tremble. He filled me to the brim, and then some. I could feel the excess dribble out onto the bed sheets.

It was over in an instant. He had given me more cum than a dozen human men could hope to match, but I still felt disappointed when the flow ended. His throbbing subsided, and I felt it begin to soften inside me. After a brief rest, he pulled his shaft free of my loins. My pussy gaped, allowing his cum to leak freely.

Lucifer climbed out of bed and took his human form again. He dressed himself, smiled warmly at me, and began to exit. I tried to get up, but my bones felt like jelly. I had yet to recover from the most intense sexual experience I'd ever had. I called out to him just before he turned the knob.

"Lucifer, wait!"

He stopped and glanced at me, still smiling. "Yes dear, what do you need?"

"What if I don't get pregnant?"

"I am certain you will. But if you don't, we will just have to try again. As many times as it takes."

I blushed deeply. "What will happen when the child is born? Am I going to have a demon baby? Will you take it away?"

"I assure you that our child will be quite human. At least on the outside. You will be free to raise that child with your husband as you see fit. I ask only two things."

"Anything, sir."

"I would like to visit my offspring on occasion. You need not tell the child the truth of his or her parentage, but I would like to see my child grow."

"And the other thing?"

"I ask that you don't provide our child with any spiritual training or guidance. Answering simple questions is fine, but I would prefer you didn't encourage any particular path. Let him or her decide what to do spiritually. Whether my spawn would serve for me or against me, or neither, let it be my child's choice."

"Yes, sir. I promise I will do my best not to influence our child's spirituality."

"Thank you, Melissa. I wish you and your family well. Feel free to call upon me whenever you have a favor to ask. I am not as distracted as some other deities, and I will try to make my terms clearer in the future."

"Thank you, sir! Um...be well?"

I felt silly immediately after saying it. I admittedly wasn't sure how to say goodbye to the devil. He nodded politely before he left, though, which I took as his approval. I rolled onto my back and fell asleep the instant my head hit the pillow.

My husband and I continued to attend church regularly, almost as a habit. At first, I felt jilted and betrayed by the Lord, but that faded. I realized that God is responsible for all of the good in the world and that it keeps him too busy to answer individual prayers. Lucifer was once an angel; I was certain God could forgive me for accepting his help.

Nine months after keeping my end of the bargain, I gave birth to a healthy baby boy. Though it was incredible cliché, I couldn't resist naming him Damien. He did not look like my husband, nor did he remotely resemble his real father. He took almost entirely after me: blond hair, blue eyes, and all. Damien's "Uncle Lou" came to visit us in the hospital to see the child at only a few hours old.

I was nervous about raising the son of Satan, but that faded in time. Damien showed himself to be one of the most polite and well-behaved children I have ever known. Though I tried my best not to influence him one way or the other, he took a strong liking to church. He read the Bible enthusiastically; it was his favorite book on into his teenage years.

"Uncle Lou" seemed disappointed, even a little sad. I think he could tell that it wasn't something I had forced though. Despite being happy that Damien had decided to become a Christian, I did feel bad for the devil. To love Jesus meant to turn his back on his father. Not that Damien knew, bless his heart.

As far as anyone knew, we were an ordinary, happy Christian family. Only my husband and I knew the secret of Catherine's recovery and Damien's conception. Many attributed our daughter's health and our son's piousness to divine intervention, and I struggled not to laugh when I heard such things. No one ever suspected that it was quite the opposite.

10 SAFARI

I pulled the door closed behind me with a heavy sigh. It had been a long day of curing minor afflictions, brewing potions, and enchanting baubles. Medical technology had advanced far enough that it came close to magic and even surpassed it in some ways. And yet, there was still such demand for my services.

Some people didn't trust medicine. Others wanted a faster, easier remedy for whatever ailed them. Why remove a wart physically when the local witch can just magic it away? There were some things science legitimately couldn't do, though. For example, I could make a laptop or MP3 player function indefinitely without ever needing a recharge. Forever batteries only exist when magic gets involved, and I'd been paid to make several every day for the past decade.

I hung my pointy hat and dark robe on

the coat rack. They served no legitimate purpose in my profession. I could perform my job just as well naked. It was the stereotypical attire of a witch, though, and my customers get confused if I don't dress the part. I'd worn a sensible tank top and jogging pants underneath. Not professional, but comfortable, and no one ever saw them. I set about undoing the many buckles on my tall black boots and stepped out of them with a happy sigh.

Martin entered the room with a warm smile. He was my heavyset, blonde househusband. Once upon a time, I'd been the one to do the cooking and cleaning while he was the provider. Our roles switched when he got laid off from the cereal factory and I started charging money to help people with their annoying problems.

"Welcome home, Abigail!"

"Just call me Abby. If I hear that name one more time, I'm going to scream."

Martin chuckled. "Rough day, huh?"

"So many people came by today! How many teenagers are going to catch herpes before these kids figure out that condoms exist?"

"Well, it is nearing the end of spring break."

"True."

"It's about to get better, though. I have enchiladas in the oven!"

I managed a tired smile. "My favorite."

"And after dinner, I'll rub your feet."

"Such a sweet man. What did I ever do to deserve you?"

Martin was quite the chef. Everything he made came out so splendidly, even without magical assistance. After a dinner of enchiladas and rice, we retired to the bedroom. He kept his promise of a foot rub, though it transitioned into cunnilingus after a while. That was another of his talents, perhaps his most impressive one. His tongue could get me bucking and screaming in no time at all.

After I got off several times, Martin crawled further up the bed. He kissed my lips, and I could feel his erection prod my thigh. I stroked his back affectionately and slipped him some tongue. My leg slid back and forth to tease his boner. The tip left a slime trail of precum across my bare flesh. When he moved himself into position, I broke the kiss.

"I'm not in much of a 'human mood' tonight, dear. Can we do something more exotic?"

Martin sat up on his knees and smiled. "Of course, sweetheart. I don't mind being transformed. It's always fun for me too, you know."

I smiled back and pointed at him. The air shimmered, and in the blink of an eye he changed. No longer a chubby human, Martin had become a lanky rabbit man. This form was lean, athletic, and lithe. Soft, white fur covered his entire body. Though much of his figure was still humanoid, his head was very much like that of a rabbit. His feet were digitigrade and rabbit-like as well. His penis mostly retained its shape, but I had enhanced its size. Eight inches of hard pink flesh stood out from his groin.

Martin examined himself and then looked at me with a wry smile. "You've been hanging out on those furry sites again, haven't you?"

I smiled back and gave a playfully dismissive wave. "So what if I have? They're a good source of inspiration."

"I'm not complaining. This way won't be awkward...like that time you turned me into a regular dog."

I laughed. "That was fun! Even if you had trouble walking on four legs, you still knew how to hump! But enough talk, my sweet. You've got two rabbit feet; it's time for you to get lucky."

Martin pounced on me and drove his hard cock into my moist slit. The rough entry was a little jarring, but he'd gotten me good and ready with his tongue, so I didn't mind. He gyrated his hips rapidly, making use of the rabbit body I'd given him.

Martin's throbbing cock pounded in and out of my tightness at an incredible speed. I was helpless to do more than lie there and moan. He gave me his full length with every powerful slam, jerking back until only the head remained inside and then surging forward until he was balls deep. I raked my fingers through the fur on his back. I could feel the rippling beneath his hot flesh; he was using every muscle in his body to satisfy me.

I came quickly, unable to hold back. Martin slowed his thrusts throughout my climax and then sped up again once my orgasmic convulsions ended. His hips moved even faster now, almost numbingly so. It took only seconds for me to cum again. This time, he wasn't far behind.

My bunny hubby buried himself as deeply as possible and then threw his head back with a moan. His stiff cock throbbed powerfully within me and planted a load of hot seed inside. I didn't have to worry about unplanned pregnancy. My ovulation cycle was on indefinite pause; I would only conceive when I chose to.

After a brief rest, Martin began to hump again, but I gently pushed him away. He took my nonverbal cue and pulled out. I pointed at him again and changed him. This time, he became a mighty anthropomorphic lion. Covered in short tan fur with a thick brown mane, I could see his thoroughly enhanced musculature. Though still human-shaped, I had enhanced his penis further. It was now a nice, thick ten inches, well beyond anything a real lion could hope to offer. I did enlarge his testicles until they were lion-sized, though.

My lover growled playfully. "Craving some variety, are we?"

"I like to think of it as going on safari."

"Roll over. If you want to breed with a lion, you'll be taken from behind like a lioness."

I laughed and rolled over for him. He was on me in an instant. I felt his thickness prod my nethers, and then he crammed it inside. I cried out at the rough entry, then again for the hard thrust that followed. He buried his entire ten inches in me with a single push. The lion man held his position for a few seconds. I could feel it throbbing so deep inside me.

Martin teased me only briefly and then pulled his hips back. When only the tip remained inside, he rammed inward again. I screamed and clenched; it was exactly what I'd hoped he would do. He couldn't match the rabbit form's speed, but the lion form offered a lot more power. He made use of it, too. Those strong hips drove his hot love spike into me with brutal force, making me yelp with every thrust.

The bed frame creaked in protest, and the headboard slapped the wall. After a few thrusts, he would further his efforts. The roughness sent sparks through my body. I couldn't help but buck back to him. My movement was rewarded with some affectionate licks to the back of my neck. His rough feline tongue made my skin tingle.

The instant I came, he slapped my ass. The rough smack only served to enhance my orgasm. He didn't slow down for me this time. The rough pounding continued throughout my climax. I writhed and shuddered beneath the hunky werelion.

"Harder! Make it hurt!"

Martin pulled out of me entirely. I was

momentarily confused, until I felt the tip of his cock touch my puckered anus. I gasped and then screamed when he pressed forward. He was slick with my juices, but not at all gentle. My ass stretched wide around his fat cock. I felt my insides cramp up a little from the far-too-sudden anal penetration, but I calmed my body with a spell.

The lion man on top of me wasted no time in resuming his savage humping. His hips smacked my ass, and those heavy balls impacted my pussy with each deep slam. I cried out every time he buried himself in my bottom. It hurt so well. My ass was on fire, and I loved every second of it.

In minutes, he clawed at the sheets and roared. With one final thrust, he emptied his sac into my bowels. The first spurt of hot cum into my body triggered my orgasm. I screamed and squirted girl cum all over those enormous balls. He pulled out of me and slapped my ass again, making me gasp.

I took a few seconds to catch my breath, then rolled over and cast the transformation spell on him again. This time, he became a werewolf. His frame combined the raw masculinity of a lion with the grace of a rabbit. The short tan fuzz had been traded in for a thick coat of fur as pure and white as freshly fallen snow. I downsized his nuts a little: lion balls wouldn't have looked quite right on a wolf. It was only a minor reduction, though. I compensated by enlarging his penis some more. It was now a full foot long. It was as thick as it had been in lion form but with a pointy tip and a knot. Just like a real wolf would have.

Martin's tail wagged excitedly when he saw himself. "This is going to be fun!"

I giggled. "Come here, wolfy. Give me that knotty cock!"

The wolf man mounted me immediately and shoved himself inside. I gasped and lifted my hips, urging his canine penis deeper into my needy pussy. His lips met mine in a kiss. It was so strange kissing someone with a wolf muzzle, but the feel of a tongue in my mouth was familiar enough.

My lover's hips rolled quickly, taking me fast and hard. He didn't use his entire length as he had before. Instead, he bred me with short, quick humps. I had taken care to give him the body temperature of a wolf as well, making his cock feel incredibly hot inside me. It was like being fucked by molten iron, and I mean that in the best possible way.

His soft fur tickled my stiff nipples, furthering my pleasure. I wrapped my arms and legs around him. My fingers curled and tightly grasped his fluffy fur. His swiftly wagging tail smacked my feet. My moans were muffled by our passionate kiss and the mouthful of wolf tongue I was suckling.

His hot girth swiftly brought me to climax. I broke the kiss to cry out and tightened my grip around him. My spasming muff encouraged him, and the hunky wolf began bucking harder. His cock probed deeper into my body, going further than most women could comfortably handle. I could feel his knot slap me with every inward push. It would soon be inside me, and the thought made me quiver.

The wolf's knot grew with every hump, swelling thicker and thicker. Once it was large enough to present a challenge – but not so big as to prevent entry – he put more force behind his pushes. The savage pounding made me cum. Just a few rough humps later, his knot slid inside. I cried out and came for him again, clenching tight around his knotted shaft.

Martin kept humping, jerking his trapped knotty cock back and forth inside me. That wide bulb of flesh ballooned rapidly, stretching me further and further. It soon reached full size, about twice the width of his shaft. My scream mingled with his howl in a loud mutual climax. My juices splashed into his fur while his hot wolf spunk coursed into my womb.

My lips met his muzzle again, and we resumed our kiss. My hands roamed along his furry back while he explored my bare flesh. His magnificent penis throbbed powerfully within me, and each pulse brought another squirt of cum. He pulled his fuzzy lips away, leaving me to gasp for air.

"Want me to try and pull out?"

"No, I could use a little break. Let's just

stay like this for a little while. We can play more when your knot shrinks."

We cuddled throughout the duration of the tie. An average wolf could remain stuck to his mate for twenty to thirty minutes. The magic I had used on Martin set him a bit above the average. His fat wolf dick shot cum into me for just over an hour before his knot finally shrank down. He slowly withdrew his softening length from my overfilled pussy. Creamy white seed spilled from my gaping snatch, making a sticky mess on the sheets.

Martin sat up on his knees to admire his handiwork. I took the opportunity to cast a spell on him. He was very handsome as a wolf; I actually regretted changing him. That feeling faded when I caught an eyeful of his new bod. I'd chosen a zebra for this transformation, and I was not disappointed. The black and white pelt really highlighted his studly physique. I had modified or enhanced the endowments of his previous forms, but there was no reason for me to do so with an equine body. The anthropomorphic zebra before me was equipped just like a real zebra would be. A foot and a half of shiny black equine flesh stood out above a pair of enormous balls. The shaft was a full two inches across for most of its length, with a ring of prepuce in the middle and a significantly thicker base. It actually looked excessively large when attached to a humanoid body, although it was still quite fetching.

My husband stared down at his cock with a surprised expression. "Isn't this a bit much?"

"For an average woman, maybe. You have to remember, dearest, that I am a witch. My pussy is magic; I can take things most women could only dream of."

"Are you sure about this?"

"Don't worry about me, honey. I wouldn't let you hurt me. Now give me that glorious dick! I want every last inch of it!"

"All right, you know best."

Martin wrapped an arm around me and kissed me. It was refreshing to smooch something with proper lips, even if they were still fuzzy. With his other hand, he guided his tremendous black tool into my sloppy snatch. I broke the kiss with a gasp when it entered me, then let out a long moan while he slid inside. Inch after inch, it disappeared into my muff. His thick meat slid well beyond the point that a nonmagical woman could physically handle. It must be such an inconvenience not being able to reposition one's cervix at will.

I felt that hot zebra dick go deeper than anything I'd ever had before. It was wonderful, even if I had to magically enlarge my pussy to enjoy it. He mashed his hips against mine and looked down. The expression he wore was an even blend of surprised and impressed. Once the shock wore off, he pulled back a few inches and started humping.

My lover's thrusts weren't as fast or hard as before, but he was very long and buried very deep. My inner depths were so sensitive each thrust sent fluttery tingles through my entire body. I moaned for him every time he pressed into me, my voice growing hoarse from all of the noise I'd already made that night. His huge balls gently impacted my bottom each time he hilted himself in me.

I wrapped myself around him and held on tight. As he grew more confident that he wasn't going to kill me with his dick, he began to pick up the pace. My moans grew louder and closer together as his thrusts came faster. It wasn't long at all before I came. My pussy rippled around his mighty shaft, but my orgasmic scream was cut short by a deep kiss.

I rode out my climax while gripping around his massive penis. Once I was done, I broke the kiss and pushed against his chest. Martin slowly pulled himself free of my loins. I could hear a loud, wet slurp when the head of his cock slipped out of my pussy. Looking down, I could see his fat black dick was streaked with cum. My vagina prolapsed a little and leaked mixed fluids like a sieve.

"Slide that big dick between my titties! I want that thing pointed at my face when it goes off."

Martin gave me a perplexed look. "I've never seen this side of you. I kind of like it."

My zebra husband obediently straddled

my chest, with a knee on either side of me. He laid his plump cock across my chest, and I squeezed my titties together around him. His hands tightly gripped the headboard, and he began to thrust. I teased my own nipples while he moved his shaft between my sensitive tits. That long dick tapped my chin at the apex of each forward thrust.

I tilted my head down and opened my mouth. Fitting my lips around his girth was a challenge, but the salty taste of semen was an acceptable reward. My lips squeegeed a layer of cum off of his member, making a mess of my lips and chin. I sucked hard on his monstrous zebra dick, tasting an exquisite blend of fresh precum, pussy juice, and still-warm spunk.

After a couple of minutes, I pulled my mouth free of his foal maker and sighed happily. I could hear him grunting above me, and I smiled. Stallions weren't known for their sexual stamina, and I hadn't made any magical modifications to the equine phallus attached to him. The poor dear had to be fighting tooth and nail to hold it in at this point. I gave the end of his cock a kiss and smiled up at him.

"Let it out, baby. Cum all over me!"

My words were enough to set his sperm free. He threw his head back with an almost painful grunt and then gave a final thrust forward. The head of his cock flared up to twice its original size and blasted my forehead with a huge wad of spunk. Three more shots followed, each accompanied by a grunt, before the last of his load trickled out onto my neck. I had expected something more like a fire hose, but he'd done pretty well anyway. My face was thoroughly coated, and he'd gotten a lot in my hair as well. Hot sperm ran down my face and neck in all directions, getting the pillow beneath me sticky.

Martin grinned down at me. "Now that is a facial!"

"There's no facial like an equine facial, you know."

"Did you learn that from furries?"

I laughed. "Where else, dear? You've just proven us right."

"I can't help but notice you said 'us' and not 'them.'"

I smiled. "After a night like this, I don't think it's possible to not count myself among their numbers."

"Just don't start using fandom terminology like 'murry purry' and 'yiff.' That would be annoying."

"Annoying or fun?"

"Annoying."

I laughed and then patted him on the belly. "Are you good to go again?"

"If I weren't, you could just use your magic."

"Of course, but do you want to play more?"

"I'm surprised you want to play more, but you know how we menfolk are. We haven't had enough until we're dead."

"Great! Stand up. I want to try something crazy."

Martin crawled off of the bed and stood next to me. "Why am I standing up?"

"Because you'd break the bed. Schwoop!" Magic doesn't require sound effects, but silly moods do. My husband changed again, this time becoming much taller. He reverted to his original body shape – chubby. However, he was now twelve feet tall and gray. His hands were enormous and strong; his feet were round and flat. His head bore the huge floppy ears, trunk, and curved tusks of an African bull elephant. This time, I had made his cock significantly smaller than the animal he resembled. I could take what a real elephant had to offer, but his current endowments represented the largest I was willing to handle. Thirty inches long, a full four and a half inches across.

Martin took a few moments to examine his new figure, mostly eyeing the colossal penis attached to his groin. "You've got to be kidding."

"I told you I was going on safari. What kind of safari would it be if I don't bag an elephant?"

"There's no way this thing would fit inside...well, anybody."

"Martin, sweetie, trust me. Trust in my powers."

"How are we even going to do it? You said yourself that I'm too heavy for the bed."

"Easy! Just hold me and pull me back

and forth across your cock. You're much stronger now; I doubt you'll even notice my weight."

"I don't get it. Wouldn't that just hurt?"

"You know pain gets me off, when it's the right kind of pain."

"Yeah, but this is..."

"If you aren't comfortable doing this, we don't have to."

"Well, I didn't say that. I'm just worried, is all."

"Quit worrying and fuck me! If you rip me in half, I'll just magic myself back together!"

He winced at the visual but then gestured for me to get up. I slid out of bed and stood in front of him, facing away. His big, strong hands gripped my sides and hoisted me into the air. I felt the bulbous head of his elephantine penis touch my slobbering pussy. A stream of pussy juice and semen ran down his length. He held me there and ground against me for a few minutes, either teasing me or working up his nerve. Maybe a little of both.

Just when I was about to beg, he pulled me down. Despite being fairly stretched already, my pussy resisted his mighty girth. All at once, the head slipped inside. My body stretched to its very limit, wrapped tightly around his cock head. I screamed until my throat burned, swimming in a beautiful cocktail of ecstasy and agony. He didn't move a muscle; he just held me in place on the end of his cock. My poor muffin squeezed around him, trying to acclimate to the girth.

Martin stroked my belly and tits with his trunk. "Are you all right, Abby?"

"M-more..."

"Are you sure? That sounded pretty painful."

"Push it into me nice and slow. Make me feel it in my chest!"

My words didn't seem to reassure him very much, but he began to sink deeper anyway. I let out a long, low-pitched cry while his tremendous cock burrowed deeper into me. I knew I would be feeling this well into next week, maybe even longer. My eyes watered. It was so thick and was probing so deep. I began to feel like splitting in half might not be a joke.

Martin finally bottomed out in me. All thirty inches were firmly buried in my vagina. I was out of breath just from taking him. He held me in place, teasing my tits while I panted. When my breathing slowed a little, he lifted me up off of his cock.

My deepest depths felt empty in his absence. He didn't leave me wanting for long, though. I rested upon his head for just an instant before he pushed me down onto him again. I let out the same low groan this time as well. I never knew it was possible to suffer and revel at the same time.

I ran my hands across my belly, feeling the obscene bulge he made in me with every thrust. I stroked his cock through my own flesh, listening to him moaning in appreciation. Each time he drew back, my tummy returned to its normal flat state. When he pressed forward, it stretched and contorted to fit his immense dick.

"Faster..."

"You can't be serious."

"Faster!"

"All right, you're the boss."

Martin tightened his grip on my body just slightly. He began to jerk me up and down his cock swiftly. I had only meant for him to do it a little faster, but I was screaming too much to say a word in protest. He moved his hips along with his arms, thrusting forward as he tugged me down. His body impacted mine hard enough to leave bruises on my thin human skin.

I couldn't do anything but scream. It hurt so much and felt so good all at the same time. I couldn't even moan properly when I came. And I did cum often. The swift, hard pounding had me squirting about once a minute. Pussy juice wasn't the only fluid pooling on the floor. I found myself crying and drooling as well. I lost count of my orgasms. It was impossible to focus on keeping track of such things with an elephant slamming me.

After a while, my throat hurt too much to scream anymore. I just whimpered instead. Martin sped up even more, apparently mistaking my quietness for boredom. The increase in pace coaxed some slightly louder whimpers out of me, but I just didn't have it in me to scream anymore.

I had no idea how much time had passed. The entire world had turned into one big blur for me. There was nothing left but me and Martin and two and a half feet of dick. I was exhausted, dehydrated, and incredibly sore. The masochistic part of me wished this would never end, but the pragmatic part wished he would finish already.

Pragmatism got its wish eventually. Martin buried himself fully and whipped his trunk through the air. I cried out weakly, a sound drowned out entirely by his mighty trumpet. That enormous cock throbbed within me and ejected a mind-blowing amount of cum. He ejaculated like a fire hose, with enough fluid pressure to actually hurt. I gasped with each shot of cum, feeling the sharp pain of his high-pressure semen impacting my tender flesh.

When he was done cumming, Martin lifted me fully off of his girth. My pussy hung open. Cum flooded from between my drooping labia. Any normal woman would have been ruined, but I could fix it with a spell. Martin laid me down on the bed. My body wouldn't stop shaking, but I could barely move otherwise. I twisted around to face him and saw the deeply concerned expression on his face. I tried to talk but could barely make a sound.

"What was that?" I tried again, this time managing a whisper.

"P-put it i-in my ass...."

Martin shook his head. "No, I think you've had enough for tonight.

Slightly disappointed, I changed him back into a human. He helped me into a comfortable position and then left the room. I was still in a daze, but as it wore off, I realized how much I was really hurting. I writhed and whimpered on the bed for a few minutes. Finally, I managed to focus and cast a spell. The pain dampened considerably, and my pussy tightened back up to its normal state. I didn't heal myself completely though. I wanted to be able to remember this in the morning.

Martin returned with a glass of ice water for me. I sat up and accepted the glass, then swiftly brought it to my lips. The water was gone in seconds. Rehydrating myself was one of the things my magic couldn't do, and my body sorely needed this.

"Need more?"

I nodded weakly. Martin took the glass and left again. He brought it back, filled with cool water. I drank the second glass just as greedily, then put it on the nightstand and flopped down. Martin crawled into bed next to me and put his arms around me. I fell into a deep sleep within seconds.

In the morning, I awoke to a sound only I could hear. I had enchanted the alarm so that it wouldn't wake Martin. I reached over to shut it off and then gently detangled myself from my husband. Standing up proved to be a challenge. Walking wasn't so easy either. I awkwardly made my way to the door, pausing to look back at the bedroom. We'd made a tremendous mess last night. I felt a little bad leaving Martin to clean it up alone. It's not like he didn't get his jollies too, though. The evidence of that was clearly visible in the crusty white stains all over the bed, the floor, and me.

A warm shower refreshed me, though it

was still hard to walk properly. I decided not to fully heal myself, at least not right away. It gave me a great excuse to brag on my husband. If anyone thought I was exaggerating, the proof was in my bow-legged gait. It took a month before I was ready to try something so crazy again, but Martin was ready and willing when the time came.

11 GRIDIRON GIRLS

Powder puff football was an annual tradition at East Dunsville High School. The senior-year football players dressed in drag and acted as cheerleaders, while the cheerleaders put on jerseys and played a game of flag football against our cross-town rivals. Chris and I were seniors this year. It was finally our turn.

I could have been a football player, and he could have been a cheerleader, but not without the mockery of our peers. The only reason he joined the football team was so that he could be a cheerleader for a day without anyone picking on him for it. I joined the cheer squad for similar reasons.

Not that people make fun of us already. I've been a complete tomboy my entire life. Cheer squad is the first time I've worn a skirt since I was too young to dress myself.

Chris is quite the opposite, he's very feminine. Not just in behavior but in looks as well. Our classmates often joke about us being a lesbian couple. I've always hated those jokes; they remind me that my breasts are too ample for me to really look boyish.

Chris has long held a secret interest in cross-dressing. He told no one but me, and I keep his secret safe. It really made him stand out from the other powder puff cheerleaders. While they had intentionally made themselves look beyond silly, he had taken his temporary position as a cheerleader quite seriously. In hose and make-up with his long hair tied back in a ponytail, he looked every bit like a flat-chested woman.

I had an edge, as well. Growing up with a single dad and three older brothers had not only made me one of the guys, but had also left me with a head full of football plays. The other cheerleaders weren't completely clueless, but playing football in the backyard and watching the game every Sunday night was a part of my upbringing. I had also taken care to wear a strap-on under my athletic uniform, which made a distracting bulge that threw off some of my opponents.

Just as I had predicted, the game was a landslide in my team's favor. The other girls all played defensively, but I happened to know some good offensive strategy. I was among the few players actually scoring, and I did so consistently. The event was just for laughs, but I played seriously. It was my only chance to play an official school game, without being ridiculed for it.

After the game, I couldn't take my eyes off of Chris. He really was beautiful in a skirt. The lesbian jokes seemed a little more believable, considering my attraction. I followed him into the boys' locker room, instead of cleaning up with the other girls. I tried to be discreet. If anyone saw me, they did nothing to stop me.

I crept up on Chris and embraced him from behind. My fake dick mashed against his bottom through our clothes. He squeaked adorably and twisted around to see who held him. Once he saw it was me, he relaxed and wiggled his thus back against my hips. We ground against each other for a few minutes, enduring the jokes of the other boys as they passed us by.

Once all of the other guys were in the shower, I reached under my boyfriend's skirt and yanked down his panties. He gasped and reached for them, but I swatted his hands away. I pulled my pants down enough to free the dildo. Then, I lifted the back of his skirt and wedged the silicone phallus between his ass cheeks.

"You're going to get us in trouble!" Despite his protests, Chris was squirming against me, not away.

"Relax, babe. All the other guys are washing up; nobody's going to see us. And even if we do get caught, they'll just be impressed when they see you taking it all like a big girl."

"All of it? That thing feels pretty big..."

"I'll bet yours is bigger." I reached around and squeezed his half-mast cock. "Ooh goody, it is! Wow, I would have put out for you earlier if I knew you were this well-equipped!"

I casually stroked my boyfriend's growing length while grinding my strap-on cock into his crevice. His meat grew harder with each passing second. His impressive, throbbing girth was quite the handful at full size. I teased the drooling head with my thumb, and felt the slippery pre-cum ooze out. For such a girly boy, he's one hell of a manly man where it counts!

Having teased him enough, I released my lover's quivering member and whirled him around to plant a fierce kiss on his lips. He moaned, and submissively offered his tongue. I slipped him some tongue as well, deepening our kiss. My hands kneaded his pert little ass. I rolled my hips, grinding my fake dick against his real one. Chris was indeed larger than the strap-on, considerably so. As much as I wanted to deflower his girly ass, I eagerly anticipated my turn on bottom as well.

I broke our kiss and gently pushed him away. He looked at me demurely, but couldn't hide the burning lust I'd ignited within him. I could see in his lovely blue eyes that he was all mine, he would do anything I told him.

"Did you put that bag in your locker, like I asked?"

Chris nodded. "Yeah, what's in it?"

"You'll see, go get it."

Chris pulled his panties completely off and walked over to his locker. He opened the door and retrieved a brown paper bag, then brought it back to me. I opened it and pulled out a tube of strawberry-flavored lubricant. Chris smiled and said, "You planned this."

"Of course I did, my dear. Do you think I wore this thing just for show?" I poured a line of slippery pink slime across the top of my silicone penis. "On your knees babe, spread that lube."

My boyfriend obediently dropped to his knees without a second thought. He wrapped his lips around the dildo and slid his mouth down its length. He didn't suck; he just used his lips and tongue to smear the lube. A moment later, he pulled his mouth free and admired his handiwork. The full length of the dildo shined with a mixture of saliva and lubricant.

"Good boy. Now, hug that bench."

"Be gentle?"

"Of course."

Chris pressed his chest and tummy flat against the bench, with his knees spread on the floor. His raised thus was an invitation I couldn't resist. I knelt behind him and lifted his shirt, exposing his girly buns. My hips moved forward ever so slowly. The toy's tip parted his cheeks and lightly grazed his anus.

Had anything up there before?"

"Just my fingers."

"Oh? How many can you fit?"

"Three."

"Then you should have no problem with

this dildo."

I pressed forward, hard. The slippery silicone glans wedged its way into my lover's tight pucker, coaxing an adorably feminine gasp from him. I eased my way deeper, watching my faux manhood disappear into him. Inch by inch, his pert bottom swallowed all that I gave. His squirms and whimpers were all the encouragement I needed.

Soon, my hips met his rump. I ground against Chris, moving the toy just slightly within him. Once I was through teasing him, I pulled back. He let out a long, low moan until I stopped with only the tip inside. Then, I pressed into him again. I made love to him, slowly but firmly. His tight butt resisted at first, but soon enough he was rocking his hips back to my thrusts.

As Chris relaxed more, I began to speed up. His vocalizations steadily rose in volume along with my pace. The possibility that the other boys might hear us, or that someone might walk by and see, sent a nervous thrill through me.

Each thrust came just a bit faster than the last. Chris clung tightly to the edges of the bench, holding on for dear life. His feminine moans and whimpers struggled to be heard over the rhythmic slap of my hips against his upturned rump.

I leaned further forward, changing the angle of my thrusts. Chris's cries deepened. I couldn't tell if I was hurting him or doing him just right, but at that moment I didn't care. With one hand I grasped his ponytail.

The other snuck around his hips to squeeze his cock. I pumped my girly boyfriend's hard meat in time with my thrusts.

"Toni, you're going to make me cum!"

"That's the idea!"

I could tell Chris was struggling to hold back. With a wicked grin, I picked up the pace. His back arched, his breathing sped up. It didn't take much longer for him to hit his peak. His body shivered and his voice rose into a cry of bliss. I could feel his thick cock pulse in my grip, and his ass flexing around my strap-on.

I milked my boyfriend for all he was worth. When he was finished, I slowed my thrusts to a stop and held my hips tight against his rump. I squeezed his still-hard cock, admiring the firmness.

Once he'd caught his breath, I pulled the dildo free. Chris sat up and smiled at me. I leaned forward to kiss him. I shamelessly tongued him while jerking his fat cock. My touch made him shiver.

Chris seemed disappointed when I broke our kiss, but watched with rapt fascination when I slid my pants further down. I unbuckled the strap-on and set it aside. Then, I took Chris's place on the bench. Torso flat on the bench, ass in the air, I eagerly awaited his touch.

I gasped in surprise when I felt his tongue on my pussy. He grasped my bottom with one hand and delicately tasted my drooling honeypot. His licks came fast and hard, each one fanning the flames of my lust. Craning my neck, I could see him stroking his thick shaft.

Chris stopped licking my muff, and I breathed a short sigh. My voice rose into a moan when his fingers took over where his tongue left off, just seconds later. He moved his head a little further up, and slid his tongue across my puckered rosebud. I clenched reflexively. The feel of his tongue dancing along my rim was alien, but not unwelcome.

His fingers explored my slick passage. First two, then three. I'd never been touched there by anyone else, the sensation of another person's fingers made me tremble. Though his enthusiasm was delightful, I could tell he'd never fingered a woman before.

"Curl your fingers. A little more. Good, now go deeper. Deeper. Ooh, now a little to the left. Ah!" I clenched tight and shivered.

Chris stopped moving his fingers and pulled his tongue away. "Are you all right?"

"God, yes! That's the spot baby, now ride it until I cum!"

Chris resumed licking my ass. At the same time, he enthusiastically stroked my g-spot. My body trembled beyond my ability to control it. His touch became stronger as his confidence grew.

There was no holding back. A powerful orgasm rocked me to my core. I screamed and clamped down on his fingers tightly. I don't know if it was the dual stimulation, the public setting, the fact that someone else was doing it, or all three; but that climax was more intense than any I had ever given myself.

My lover teased me for just a moment longer, then pulled his fingers free of my wetness. I wasn't left wanting long. A trickle of cool lubricant ran down my ass crack, soon joined by an inquisitive finger. I pressed back to him, then let out a gasp as that finger slipped inside.

While I was distracted by an intruding finger, Chris moved up behind me. His thick glans parted my folds and slid into my sopping wet pussy. He'd applied some of the strawberry lube while I wasn't looking. Combined with my pussy juice, it allowed him to enter me quite easily.

Thanks to his fingering, it wasn't too much more of a stretch to get his incredible girth into me. I held the edges of the bench tightly. Each little push from him coaxed a soft yelp from my lips. He was stretching me further than any of my dildos could, and going deeper than I ever went on my own.

I began to feel uncomfortable once he got most of it in, but I said nothing. I wanted to find how much of his impressive cock I could take. It wasn't long before he had the full nine inches in me. He held it deep inside, letting me feel his heartbeat.

I felt a second finger slip into my bum. Chris immediately distracted me from that stretching feeling by humping. His thrusts were slow and deliberate. Each push made me cry out softly. I clenched tight around his huge tool, reveling in the feel of him.

Suddenly, he pulled out. At first, I was afraid he was already finished. Then, I felt him spread his fingers to open my ass up more. He guided his cock between my cheeks and wedged just the head inside. After applying a little more lubricant, he eased his way inside.

I was hyperventilating. His dick stretched me wide. It felt even bigger in the back door than in the front. My eyes watered, but it hurt in a good way. Not that I was about to complain, regardless. He sat still and played nice while I penetrated him, and I intended to do the same. Turnabout is fair play, after all.

Chris managed to get his full length into my ass. I was impressed with myself for handling so much meat on my first time taking it up the bum. I could feel each throb of his magnificent rod even more acutely now.

My lover pulled back by just a few inches, and then pushed back inside. He settled into a slow, easy rhythm. I exhaled sharply every time his hips met my butt. So big, so deep! My juices trickled down my thighs.

I knew we didn't have a lot of time, so I tried my best to relax. With some effort, I managed to unclench a little. Chris took this as a sign to speed up, and immediately did so. My cries rose in volume. He upped his pace a little at a time. Each thrust was just a bit harder than the last.

My entire body trembled. He was tearing me apart in the best of ways. I didn't care that it hurt, it was too hot to let something like that bother me. I timed my flexes, squeezing tight when he pulled out and trying to relax when he pushed in.

Chris leaned over my back and grabbed my shoulders. His thrusts came very hard and fast now. I could feel his big, heavy balls slap my wet snatch with every slam. I screamed, no longer caring if anyone heard me. The locker room was bound to smell like sex now, anyway. I knew there would be no hiding what we were doing.

The other boys came out of the shower while Chris was pounding me. I did my best to ignore the laughter and jokes. Despite my best efforts at pretending not to care, I couldn't stop myself from blushing. The attention didn't break my boyfriend's rhythm for even a second. His thrusting hips helped keep my mind occupied.

The guys got dressed and left the locker room, giving us some privacy at last. Now alone with Chris, I gave up on holding back at all and allowed myself to get loud. My volume only rose further when I climaxed. Shaking and screaming, I clenched tight around my lover. Chris thrust harder to compensate for the extra tightness. I knew my butt would be sore later, but I didn't care.

Chris didn't last much longer. Just seconds after my orgasm, he pushed all the way inside and held himself there. An adorably feminine cry escaped his lips, and jets of hot seed erupted into my rear. Each shot of cum was accompanied by an exquisitely powerful throb of his mighty tool.

I felt more than a little disappointed when he pulled out. The emptiness was jarring, I wanted to keep him inside me forever. Still, I knew someone could come looking for us at any minute. Chris stepped back and stripped out of his cheerleader outfit. I stood and kissed him on the lips, then peeled off my own uniform.

Chris and I had the shower to ourselves. We took the opportunity to wash each other a bit more intimately than we would have with the others there, but we still tried not to take a long time. I scrubbed him, he scrubbed me, then I cleaned my strap-on, and we got out. I didn't realize until afterwards that I'd left my clothes in the girls' locker room. Chris realized the problem around the same time I did, and smiled.

"Don't worry; I brought an outfit for you." He pulled some clean clothes out of his duffel bag. My clothes.

"You're a life saver! Where did you even get those?"

"You know all those times you come over to swim, then walk home in your swimsuit? I kind of have a lot of your clothes at my house, now. You can pick them up whenever."

I laughed. "I keep forgetting about that. I'm glad I never did, though."

"I don't know. It would be kind of entertaining to watch you scamper over to the girls' locker room, naked."

"Nonsense, I'd just take your clothes."

Chris glanced at the door and blushed. "Think anyone knows what we did in here?"

"Who cares? We both got laid today. If

anyone wants to give us a hard time for that, they're just jealous."

We held hands and left the locker room together. People did say things, but we took it in stride. We had each other, no matter what dumb jokes our classmates wanted to make.

12 BLUE SCREEN OF DESIRE

Computers have never been my strong suit. So, whenever mine breaks down, I know it's beyond my capability to fix it. The unresponsive blue screen is about as repairable as the aftermath of a nuclear explosion – that is, from my perspective. That's what Nick is for.

Nick and I met in high school. He always struck me as the hopeless, perpetual virgin type, unceremoniously walled into the friend zone by every girl he talks to. He wasn't ugly, but I couldn't really call him attractive either. He was a scrawny little nerd, as unsexy as he was nonthreatening. More like a kitten than a man.

We remained in contact throughout college and beyond. He had a real knack for computers, but it wasn't his passion. He'd taken on a job as a curator at a local museum. It was a job he really loved, and it paid enough for him to live on, but it certainly wasn't impressive.

As many times as he'd fixed my computer for me, I felt confident he could thrive in a well-paying tech job. But he was choosing to follow his heart, which was admirable in its own way. His lack of professional interest also netted me free tech support whenever I needed it, which was definitely a plus.

Nick seemed annoyed with me this time. He told me something about my browser toolbars; I didn't really listen. He'd given this speech before. I couldn't imagine using my computer without toolbars. I also can't tell the difference between the good ones and the bad ones. It's easier to just play dumb and let him sort it out. For some reason, he likes to delete all of my toolbars when he fixes my computer.

While Nick was busy at the computer desk, I went upstairs. Nick was always such a nice guy, and I wanted to thank him for fixing my computer as many times as he has. A special sort of 'thank you.' Something that might just change his life.

I stripped out of my comfortable house clothes, even my underwear. I picked some sexy clothes out of my closet and re-dressed myself in a far more provocative manner. Long, dark stockings and a black garter belt were all I wore on my lower body. I neglected to put on panties; they'd have to come off soon anyway. I wrapped my torso in a black corset, adorned with pink lace. It worked like a push-up bra, making my ample breasts look even more squeezable. I made some final adjustments in the mirror and then headed downstairs.

Nick was still busy on the computer. I wrapped my arms around him from behind, pulling the back of his head into my cleavage. He barely seemed to notice. I couldn't tell if he was purposefully ignoring me or was just wrapped up in what he was doing.

"Feel like taking a break?" I said.

"No need. I'm almost finished."

"Oh, good. I have something special in mind to thank you."

"What's that?"

I let go of Nick and stepped around to the side of the computer chair. He glanced over at me and went wide-eyed. I could see his eyes exploring my body until his glasses fogged up. His reaction made me grin.

"I'll be waiting upstairs when you're finished, computer guy."

I made my way back to the stairs, swinging my hips just in case he was watching. Upon my return to the bedroom, I made myself comfortable on the bed. I was positioned so that he would have a clear view of my trimmed, heart-shaped bush the instant he walked in the door.

I wasn't left waiting long. Just ten minutes after I lay down, Nick joined me in the bedroom. His eyes met mine and then drifted down to my crotch. I could see the desire in his gaze, but not a hint of shyness.

Nick peeled out of his clothes with a little more confidence than I expected. At first, I thought his lust had emboldened him. Then, he took off his underwear. That was something I hadn't expected either. The meat log hanging between his legs was all the confidence any man could ever need.

My lover didn't hesitate to climb onto bed. He buried his face between my thighs and got to work. Nick clearly knew what he was doing. His tongue moved in strong direct strokes. The lewd massage sent powerful tingles through my entire frame. My back arched, and my toes curled.

"You've done this before."

Nick looked up from my crotch with a sly grin. "You're not the first to thank me this way."

My lover resumed devouring my slick snatch. His licks were even more enthusiastic now and brought greater sensations along with them. I grabbed him by the hair and humped his face. It no longer mattered how sexy or unsexy he was: he had skill! I regretted not offering myself to him sooner. If only I'd known of his capabilities.

Tongue, lips, and even teeth teased my most sensitive places with wondrous talent. I'd never been eaten so well in my life. Suddenly, the incredible sensations stopped. Nick sat up and wiped his mouth on the back of his hand. I glanced down at his crotch and quivered. His little pony went full horse while I wasn't looking.

"I'm kind of big. Can you handle me?"

"Oh, I think so. It'll be like my first time all over again."

I reached for the nightstand drawer to retrieve a condom, but Nick was already climbing off of the bed. He picked up his pants and pulled a magnum condom out of one pocket. I watched him roll the clear latex onto his throbbing pole. My lust grew stronger with each passing second.

"You brought rubbers to fix my computer?"

"It's always a good idea to have one handy."

"Can't argue with that."

Nick joined me in bed once more. He crawled towards me on all fours, his mighty dong swinging between his legs with each little movement. Soon, we were face to face. I felt his latex-clad cock head brush my petals. My lips met his in a passionate kiss. I reached up to remove his glasses and placed them on the nightstand, all without breaking lip lock.

The tip of Nick's broad organ parted my folds and wedged its way inside. I moaned hotly into the kiss. My pussy stretched further than ever before to accommodate his girth. I could feel it throbbing inside me; the sensation gave me chills.

My lover was very gentle and took his time sliding into me. Inch after inch of hard cock slid into my slippery muff. He gave me the full ten inches with one slow push. I felt his hips mash against mine. His pole throbbed exquisitely inside me, and I flexed in response. He was in deep enough to hurt, but I didn't care.

I was allowed to savor his full length for a few seconds, and then he began to pull back. Despite the mixture of natural and artificial lubricants, there was a very distinct tugging sensation. It had been years since I felt so tight.

After pulling halfway out, Nick slid back inside. I broke the kiss to let out a soft moan. He settled into a slow, easy rhythm. I writhed beneath him, reveling in the sensations he gave.

His hips moved with an infuriating slowness. I begged for more without saying a word, but he ignored my pleas. Each tender push fanned the flames of my lust. I had never felt so needy before. My pussy was wetter than it had ever been.

"Faster!" I said.

"Don't you want to make it last?" said Nick.

As much as I did want to make it last and enjoy the feeling, I didn't feel like I could. "Please, I need it hard!"

Nick picked up the pace considerably. For such a scrawny guy, he really had some power in his hips! I cried out softly each time he drove into me. I saw sparks flashing before my eyes. My hips moved of their own accord, reflexively meeting his every thrust.

It was more than I could take. After just a few blissful minutes, it hit me. I arched, screamed, and raked my nails down Nick's back. He held himself deep inside while I clenched. When my orgasm subsided, he pulled his throbbing tool free.

I sat up on my elbows. "Did you finish?"

"No, I'm not quite there yet. Are you good to go again? I can finish myself if you don't want to."

"No way! That was one of the most incredible sex I've ever had. To let you leave without getting you off would be criminal. How do you want me?"

"Doggy style would be nice."

"Doggy it is."

I rolled over and got on my hands and knees. Nick mounted right away. He pressed his thick tool into me slowly, coaxing a long, deep moan from my lips. Once it was in, he began to buck violently. I yelped with each hard thrust.

Nick's savage humping sent shock waves of bliss through my body. I rocked back to his every move, craving him like no man ever before. My arms felt like wet noodles, trying desperately to support my upper body. After just a few minutes, they gave out. I did a face plant into the pillows, with my ass still held up in the air for Nick to tame.

I was helpless to do more than lie there, panting and moaning. My lover had complete control over my body, and I loved every second of it. I barely had to move at all. His mighty thrusts pushed me forward, and it was all I could do to slide back to my original position before the next push.

I was lost in the sea of carnal delight. The motion of the ocean and the size of the boat were both so mind-bendingly decadent. The combination sent waves of irresistible bliss crashing through my trembling form.

I fought for a modicum of control – for just a few more seconds of resistance. I wanted to badly make this feeling last forever. Despite my best efforts, I just couldn't hold on. With an arch and a shriek, I clamped down on Nick's hard tool and shuddered my way through another breathtaking orgasm.

Nick wasn't far behind. When I came, he picked up the pace significantly. Each brutal slam tore a quiet scream from my lips. Less than a minute after my climax, he thrust as deep as possible and groaned. I could feel his thick organ throbbing inside me. I closed my eyes and imagined him filling the condom like a water balloon.

We rested for a short while. I could hear Nick panting above me. After catching his breath, he pulled out of my well-used pussy. I flopped down on my side and watched him remove the prophylactic. My imagination had definitely exaggerated his volume, but there was still an impressive amount of guy-goo in the rubber.

After tossing the used condom into my bedside trash can, Nick laid down next to me. I rolled over and wrapped my arms around his sweaty naked body. I clung to the man possessively, still feeling aftershocks.

After taking a long moment to relax, I spoke, "Nick, I want you to be my boyfriend."

"I take that to mean the sex was good?"

I laughed. "It's more than that. I mean yes, the sex was incredible. You're also smart, funny, and sweet. Most of the guys I've taken to bed aren't half the man you are, and I mean that in more than one way."

"How many guys have you been to bed with?"

"Don't worry about it. I always play safe and I get myself checked once a month, so I'm squeaky clean."

"That's not what I meant. I was just curious because you sound experienced."

"Well, I am. But I mean it when I say you're the best I've ever had. We're already good friends, so I don't see why either of us needs anyone else. If you can stand having a girlfriend who sucks at using a computer, that is."

Nick laughed. "Oh, I think I'll manage to teach you someday."

13 A WOMAN'S TOUCH

With a heavy sigh, I pulled the door shut behind me. I was sticky and sore in places I don't care to mention. I could hear Angela in the kitchen, but I went upstairs instead of greeting her. A long day of work had left me unpleasantly fragrant. I reeked of sweat and Astroglide. A long, hot shower would set me right and improve my scent.

The adult film industry might look glamorous from the outside, but it isn't so different from a regular job. Granted, my job is to have sex on camera, but the novelty of that wears off quickly. I do as I'm asked, I get paid. Rinse, repeat. This was most certainly not what I thought I'd be doing after college, but there isn't a lot of demand for a philosophy major in the workplace.

The porn films paid the bills, which was reason enough for me to stay the course. I can tolerate getting slammed by a bunch of guys, even if straight sex isn't quite my cup of tea. Though my on-camera vocalizations often suggest otherwise, men really do nothing for me. My director, Scotty, once promised he'd cast me in a lesbian film when he finds one I'm "right" for. I wouldn't question the casting decisions of a professional porn director, but I often found myself wishing I could get paid to do what feels natural.

I washed myself thoroughly, ensuring I cleaned every last bit of spunk and sweat and lube from my nooks and crannies. The hot water was very relaxing, and made me keenly aware of how tired I actually was. Some play time with my soul mate and a good night's sleep would have me feeling right as rain.

A beautiful voice echoed up the stairwell. "Brandy! Dinner is ready!"

I turned off the spigot and stepped out of the shower stall. After drying off, I headed downstairs in the nude. Angela and I were both very comfortable with our bodies. We only put something on if it was cold or we were going out. Our curtains remained closed at all times to keep out prying eyes. The constant nakedness made it easy to sneak in a grope or a squeeze here and there.

Angela was wearing nothing but an apron. I snuck up behind her and grasped her plush bottom with both hands. My lover gasped and wiggled her delightful hips. She had just the slightest hint of pudginess to her build. She certainly wasn't fat, but her curves were a bit more rounded than mine and she had softness in places I didn't.

My hands kneaded her plush tush for several minutes. Then, I knelt behind her. She was leaning forward just enough to give me an eyeful of her glistening slit. I pressed my face forward. My tongue lashed across her pussy in swift, ravenous strokes. I'd barely gotten a taste of her before she pushed me away with her foot.

"Knock that off. If you eat too much pussy, you'll spoil your appetite! Save it for dessert."

I stood and licked my lips. "Ooh, yum. Can I have it with whipped cream?"

"Sure! Just don't try to shove the can into me this time. I'm not stretchy like you."

I laughed. "Give it time, darling."

She turned around and kissed me on the lips. Then, she shed her apron and fully bared herself. We made our way to the table, where she'd already laid out two plates of food. My nostrils were treated to the delightful scent of grilled chicken and steamed broccoli.

"So, how was work?" Angela asked whilst impaling a piece of broccoli on her fork.

"Long and hard," I answered playfully. "I had to shoot so many scenes today. They even had me do double-vaginal with a couple of Italian guys."

"Italian? How exotic! What was that like?"

"Meh. After a while, all wieners start to feel the same. I was actually feeling numb by the time they shot that scene."

"They're working you too hard! Your poor little pussy deserves a break."

"I could use a vacation, but relaxation doesn't pay the bills. I just wish they'd let me do a lesbian scene every now and then."

"I can help you with that. We'll do our own lesbian scene after dinner. No men, no cameras. Just you, me and our love. Oh, and some toys."

I smiled. "I love you, Angie. You're all the woman I need."

We made small talk over dinner. Once we were done eating, I helped Angela wash the dishes. Then, she took my hand and led me upstairs. When we reached the bedroom, she bent me over the side of the bed.

Angela knelt and attacked my upturned backside right away. Her lovely hands clutched my cheeks, and her tongue wriggled through my crevice. The tip of her wonderful pink oral organ tickled my puckered anus. I clenched reflexively, but her relentless licks relaxed me.

When my rosebud stopped fighting her, she pressed her tongue inside. I moaned softly and welcomed the intrusion. While her tongue swirled and wiggled its way deeper, her fingers teased my overworked pussy. I appreciated the effort, but the touch of her fingers didn't do much to help me along. My front door was completely worn out; her teasing tickles got zero response.

Angela made sweet love to my bum with her tongue for several minutes. The treatment was definitely working. I was desperately horny in no time. Suddenly, the delightful oral pleasure ceased. I looked back and whimpered, which earned me a playful swat on the behind.

Angela stood and walked to the closet. She dug through our toy box, and then retrieved a reasonably sized strap-on. I held my position, eagerly awaiting her return. Angela grabbed a tube of lubricant and made her way back to the bedside.

I felt the silicone phallus slide between my cheeks and pressed my hips back into it. Angie snapped the cap off of the lube and poured cold, slippery slime across the length of the toy. Her hips rolled slowly, smearing the slick sex jelly all over the toy and my bum.

Once everything was nice and slick, I felt the tip of the dildo prod my anus. Angela gave me a couple of playful pokes before shoving the toy inside. I gasped and clenched around the slippery intruder. The toy slipped deeper, little by little.

My butt hadn't been given any attention on the set. The slow, tender buggering was a very soothing change of pace. Angela eased inward, further and further. Each soft push sent a spark of arousal through me.

At long last, my lover's hips pressed against my bottom. I pushed back, driving her silicone cock as deep as possible. She briefly ground against me, then pulled back.

Once only the faux glans remained inside, she eased forward again.

Her movements were teasingly slow. The pace was at once relaxing and maddening. I wiggled and clenched to signal for her to go faster, but she either didn't take the hint or ignored my non-verbal request.

Angela's hands clasped my shoulders. She kneaded my flesh, coaxing a moan of approval from me. Her hands roamed along my upper back, caressing and stroking in ways only she knew how. I practically melted into the sheets, now content to let her do as she pleased.

Those heavenly hands made their way down my back ever so slowly. She took her sweet time in massaging me. Her touch drove away every little bit of tenseness inside me. My lover's touch moved steadily lower and lower. All the while, her hips maintained the same slow and steady pace.

When Angela's hands reached my hips, everything changed. The massage ceased instantly as she gripped my hips tight. Her thrusts came hard and fast now. Her hips loudly slapped my upturned bottom with every swift hump. The sudden shift had me panting like a bitch in heat. As refreshing as the gentleness had been, rough sex was what would get me off.

Pleasant tingles ran up and down my spine with each delightfully rough push. I clenched tight around the swiftly moving silicone phallus. My squeezing further enhanced the wonderful sensations. My cries steadily rose in volume and pitch as an orgasm crept ever closer.

Angela sharply slapped my tush. "Cum for me, you little slut!"

My lover's urging wore down the last of my resistance. I threw back my head and let out a scream. Hot love ran down my thighs. Angela stopped moving and just held the toy inside while I writhed. Just as the last aftershocks were dying down, Angela gave me a few more quick jabs. I cried out softly with each thrust. It was just enough to extend my good feelings by a few seconds.

I uttered a quiet groan when my lover pulled the dildo free. I was sad to feel it leave, but in all honesty I was too tired for a second round. I stood and turned, then kissed Angela on the lips. She returned the smooch, reaching around to grab my ass.

Angela broke the kiss after just a few seconds, and playfully spanked me. "Did you get a facial today?"

"No, I just did a bunch of vaginal scenes."

"Well, I can fix that. Get on your knees; I'll give you all the facial you need."

"You always take such good care of me."

I smiled and knelt in front of Angela. She grabbed me by the hair and pulled my face against her crotch immediately. I didn't hesitate to wedge my tongue into her pink. Angie was fond of cleanliness. Her attentive grooming ensured that I was always an eager carpet-muncher for her. I wiggled and undulated my tongue in alternating patterns. I did my best to be unpredictable, to keep her off-guard. I clutched her buttocks in my hands and reveled in devouring her muff.

Her grip loosened slightly, giving me just enough freedom to grip her clit between my lips. I hummed and sucked. The tip of my tongue flicked across her pink pearl in swift strokes. One of my hands abandoned her bottom in favor of driving a pair of fingers into her slavering snatch. I went straight for her G-spot and rode it hard.

Angela shuddered and bucked her hips. "Damn, girl! Aren't you going to take your time and savor me?"

I responded by humming more loudly. My fingers and tongue moved even faster. Angela's grip tightened and her moans grew louder. Her entire body quaked with pleasure. It always made me feel good about myself to be able to have this kind of effect on her. Her warm fluids dribbled down my chin, along my neck and across my breasts.

Suddenly, Angela pushed me away. "Open wide, here it comes!"

I leaned back, opened my mouth and closed my eyes. I could hear the slick sound of Angela frantically stroking her mound. The noise was soon drowned out by an ecstatic scream. Wet warmth splashed across my face. Angela painted me with her hot love honey. Her pussy squirted stripe after stripe of thickened fluid. I could tell from her volume that she hadn't masturbated today. Only one shot actually made it into my mouth. I savored her sweetly musky flavor.

The feel of Angela's hot muff slime all over my face and hair was an incredible turn on. I've been on the receiving end of facials before, but it's just not the same with a guy. This really wasn't something Angie and I did often enough. I opened my eyes and immediately had to re-close the left one. A rope of girl-cum threatened to blind me otherwise.

I allowed Angela a moment to catch her breath, then stood and kissed her. I slid my tongue into her mouth and gave her the cum I'd been saving. Her eyes went wide, but she accepted the re-gift and swallowed it. Snowballing always seemed to surprise her, no matter how many times I did it.

We mashed our naked breasts together and kissed for several minutes. When our lips parted, my lover licked her own emissions from my face. The feel of her warm tongue made my flesh tingle. As turned on as I was, though, I couldn't wait to get some rest.

"I think I'm going to need another shower."

"Can I come with?"

"Of course!"

Our shower was brief. Angela tried to coax some more play time out of me, but I was too sleepy to really crave it. I was horny, but fatigue beats out arousal. She seemed a little disappointed, so I promised to make it up to her in the morning. Oh, how excited she was to wake up with my crotch in her face.

14 SIREN'S SONG

I drove slowly through a parking lot, eyes peeled for a particular vehicle. When the gray Celica came into view, I parked my Jeep in the spot next to it. I ran my fingers through my dark hair and climbed out of my vehicle. An old white man sat on the car's hood, his wild white hair blowing in the wind.

I'd been an amateur explorer for years. Following treasure maps was my favorite hobby. I rarely found anything of value, but the fun was in the journey. My job prohibited me from getting too far away from home, but Craigslist had made it easy enough to find adventure locally.

I approached the elderly man. He whipped around and looked at me with the craziest green eyes I've ever seen. Then he smiled, showing off all three of his teeth. Just as I began to wonder if I'd approached the wrong person, he held up a piece of paper. It was yellowed with age, neatly folded, and tattered around the edges.

"Here to buy the map, sonny? You're Juan, right?"

"Yes, that's me."

I dug the money out of my pocket and handed it to him. He accepted my payment and handed me the map. Before I could open it to have a look, he grabbed my wrists and pulled me close.

"Beware the birds."

"What birds?" He released me and pointed to a nasty looking scar, then cackled. "The birds! They lie to your eyes and try to trick you, but don't believe what you see! They might look pretty, but they're not what they seem!"

"What the hell are you talking about?"

"Why do you think I'm selling my map? I never found that treasure, you know! The birds, they protect it! They won't let you come close! They try to play games with your head. If you resist, they'll fight you!"

"I'll keep that in mind, thanks."

"Take a gun! Take a bunch of guns! And a knife! Don't let the birds get you!"

"All right, then. I'll watch out for those birds."

I got back in my Jeep, feeling incredibly uncomfortable. The old white man was staring at me, which did little to abate my discomfort. I unfolded the map and glanced at it. The treasure was marked near a local public beach. I folded the map and turned the ignition key. The old guy was really starting to get to me; I decided to look at the map in more detail elsewhere.

A short drive later, I was in another parking lot closer to the beach. I opened the map again and took a closer look. The "X" was placed on a small patch of sand on the other side of a rocky outcropping, blocked from the beach by cliffs. I would have to do some swimming to get there. I climbed into the back of my Jeep and pulled curtains over the windows to change into my bathing suit privately.

I exited my vehicle clad in swim trunks. A dive knife was strapped to my calf in a sheath. I also wore a small, waterproof backpack carrying some equipment, including the map. I had only a few lightweight tools with me. I could come back to the Jeep if I needed something sturdier.

The old man's warning echoed in my head as I walked along the hot sand. I couldn't help but feel a little nervous every time a seagull flew over me. I stared at the map while walking, trying to mentally plot a course for my swim. Once I neared the cliffs, I tucked the map safely into my pack again.

The water was chilly, but not unbearably cold. It wasn't a very long swim, but finding the cove was tricky. The rocks conspired to block it from view, even from the water. I never would have found it if I weren't looking for it.

A beautiful voice graced my ears when I neared the cove. It distressed me that someone had found this place before me, but I assured myself that she most likely hadn't found the treasure. I couldn't understand what she was singing, but it had an intoxicating effect on me.

I reached the sand at last, unable to wipe the goofy smile from my face. The patch of beach was smaller than I'd imagined. It was simply a tiny, sandy gap in the rocks. I could see a cave on the far end, though. The treasure was undoubtedly there.

Something else caught my attention, halting my progress toward the cave. My silly grin only grew now that I could see who was singing. The most beautiful white woman I'd ever seen was standing on the beach, singing her enchanting song. She wore a flowing white garment that hid absolutely nothing. Her fantastic breasts were fully exposed, and I could see her muff every time the wind picked up.

My swimming trunks suddenly felt very uncomfortable. I shed my pack and knife, and then peeled out of my swimsuit to fully expose my brown skin. My cock was growing firm already. I approached the singing woman, my erection bobbing in front of me with each step. I don't know what I expected to happen, but I'd be cheating myself if I didn't speak to this vision of loveliness.

"Hello, beautiful."

The woman stopped singing and smiled at me. Those perfectly pouty lips of hers nearly made me melt. "Hello. I do so love company; it gets ever so lonely here."

"My name is Juan. What can I call you?"

"Names are not important. It is just you and I here; we needn't burden ourselves with such trite gestures."

"If you say so. What is a beautiful woman like yourself doing out here all alone?"

"Singing, of course. I have long hoped that my song of yearning would bring me a strong, handsome, brave man! And now it has, I don't have to be lonely anymore."

I reached out and placed my hands on her shoulders. "You don't ever have to be alone again, mamacita. I'm here for you."

She wrapped her arms around me and kissed me forcefully. It was a little startling, but I found myself unable to pull away. Our tongues wrestled, and our moans mingled. Her hands roamed all over my naked body, and my hands explored hers. She squeezed my cock in one hand, the other teased my butt. I broke the kiss when I felt a finger tickle my hole.

"Hey now, that's getting a little weird."

"You are an explorer, aren't you? I am an explorer, too."

"That cave is off limits!"

She giggled. It was a delightful sound that almost made me change my mind on the spot. "Maybe later, then."

"Yeah, maybe...later. I mean, no. I don't...maybe."

For some reason, I couldn't put my thoughts together. I most certainly didn't want to be on the receiving end of any ass-play today. But at the same time, I felt compelled to agree because she wanted me to. I was a little alarmed by the conclusion, but rationalized that I was just horny enough to become suggestible.

The mysterious woman kissed me again, just as fiercely as last time. Her hands stayed free of my rump, and I repaid her the same courtesy. After a few moments, I broke away from her lips and kissed my way down her neck.

Her breasts were immaculate. Truly, this was the most beautiful rack I had ever laid eyes upon. Her skin was smooth and milky, like fine porcelain. I paused, momentarily. Was she this pale a minute ago? I could distinctly remember her having a slight tan. I ignored it as a trick of my imagination and tasted those lovely breasts.

The feel of her smooth flesh on my tongue made my penis ache with need. I licked and kissed all over her mammaries. I teasingly avoided her nipples at first, though. Once the sight of her perky, erect nips began to mock me, I wrapped my lips around one and suckled. She rewarded me with a melodious moan and tickled my cheeks with soft feathers.

My eyes went wide. Feathers? Where could she have gotten feathers? I pulled my mouth free with a pop and stood back. The woman before me was not human. Her arms and thighs were coated in green feathers. She lacked hands, her arms ended in wings instead. Her lower legs were devoid of feathers. Instead, they were narrow pillars of dark brown flesh that ended in hawk-like talons. Her belly, chest, and the lower part of her face were still human-looking, if quite pale. The top of her head bore green feathers instead of the dark hair she'd had earlier.

Her eyes were beady and black, like a bird's.

"W-what the hell are you?"

She smiled. "Did I startle you, love? My apologies. Come, kiss me some more. Make love to me, here in the sand."

"But, you're...you're not...I don't..."

"Don't you find me beautiful?" She looked directly into my eyes, and I could see the beautiful human who'd been there before. "You do think I'm pretty, don't you?"

It was a struggle to pull my eyes from hers. The instant I stopped looking at her face, I could see her as a bird-monster again. She lifted my chin with the end of a wing and made me look into her eyes again. Beautiful, blue eyes. Nothing at all like the bird eyes I'd just seen a moment ago. Something was very wrong with my head.

"Tell me I'm pretty!"

"You are...the most beautiful woman I've ever seen in my life." I hadn't meant to say it, but I found myself believing it afterwards. "Please, let me make love to you. I need you like I've never needed anyone before."

She smiled and kissed my lips. "You will have me, my dear."

The illusion vanished. Her eyes were black and beady; her skin was pale and feathery. For some reason, I still found her incredibly attractive. The bird-lady got comfortable on the sand, flat on her back with her legs open wide. I could see a gap in her feathers, filled in with a patch of fluffy down.

I knelt in front of my inhuman lover, cautious not to mash her tail under my knees. I caressed her body, feeling warm flesh and soft feathers. Assuming the downy patch to be where she kept her crotch, I guided my straining cock. The tip of my shaft found a slick, wet opening. I slid inside easily.

My sensitive dick was immediately set alight by unbelievably intense tingles. Her pussy was unlike anything I'd ever felt before. No human woman could ever hope to compare! I dug my fingers into the sand and then began to swiftly ravish my avian partner. She let out adorable little gasps and cries of pleasure with every swift buck of my hips. Her wings caressed my bare back.

"Do you love me?"

The question broke my rhythm momentarily. "What? We just met! And you aren't even human!"

Our eyes met. She didn't disguise herself, this time. She knew she didn't need to. "Do you love me?"

"I-I love you!" It felt good just to say it. My brain flooded my body with feel-good chemicals the instant those words crossed my lips. "I love you, I love you, I love you, I love you!"

She smiled, rewarding my obedience even further. "Will you stay here and be mine forever?"

"I will! I'll never leave, I promise!"

"Such a sweet, obedient man! Please say you'll be mine. All mine, forever and ever."

"I'm yours, baby! There will never come a day when I don't belong to you!"

I felt bewildered by the words coming out

of my mouth. Something was definitely wrong with me. However, I couldn't bring myself to even think of leaving her now. The siren was beautiful beyond description, and I really and truly felt love for her. I may not have loved her before, but I was in love with her now. It was a privilege to belong to such a wonderful creature.

"You are a very good man. You deserve a reward for such eager and attentive obedience." She made eye contact again, sending chills down my spine. "Cum!"

What a strange coincidence that she would say such a thing at just the perfect moment. I hadn't even felt close to an orgasm, but I must have been. The very instant she spoke that word, an intense climax hit me out of nowhere. I arched my back and buried my cock fully in her slavering mound. I cried out and shivered, rocked by the most intense orgasm I'd ever had. I spilled an unbelievable load of seed into her. It was like I'd cum three times simultaneously. Just as I began to fear I'd never stop squirting jism, it was over.

I rested for a few seconds and then sat up on my knees to observe my handiwork. Her pubic down was a cummy mess. My excessive load dribbled out freely and oozed into her tail feathers. Something else caught my eye. A rather large penile erection jutted out of her feathers, just above her pubic down. It was ten inches long and at least an inch and a half across. The shaft maintained a consistent girth along its gently curved length, but toward the end it tapered to a pointed tip.

I didn't gawk. For some reason, I felt as though I'd known the whole time. I wanted to be shocked, but couldn't. She was beautiful; every part of her was beautiful. Even her huge, freaky, bird-monster penis. She collected a dollop of semen with a wing-tip and brought it to her mouth for a taste.

"My, how flavorful you are! I will have to finish you with my mouth next time."

"Yes, love. Whatever love wants."

"I'm quite worked up. Regular sex just isn't enough for me to finish, you know? Could you be a dear and..."

Before she could even finish her request, I turned away from her and got on my hands and knees. She got up and came closer then caressed my bottom with her feathers. I don't know what she was going to ask of me, specifically. But I knew what she would like, and I intended to give it to her.

"My oh my. Are you saying your cave is open for exploration, now?"

"My body is yours, my love. I exist only to bring you pleasure. Make love to me, give me your everything, and mark me as your love-slave forever."

That was definitely an odd thing for me to say. I meant every word, but the analytical portion of my brain asserted that I wouldn't normally say such a thing. I began to feel just the tiniest suspicion that the siren might be somehow controlling my mind. But that was just silly. I pushed the thought from my mind and assured myself that this is just what love feels like.

The siren took some time to explore my body with her feathered caress. I kept my eyes locked on the sand, submissively. I couldn't see her face, but I could feel her smiling. I knew she was pleased with my submissiveness. I wiggled my rump from side to side, inviting her to enter me without saying a word.

Hot flesh slid between my cheeks. I braced myself, ready for painful penetration. The first push into my virgin ass was a pleasant surprise, though. I felt nothing but pleasure. She felt even better inside me than I'd felt inside her. I pressed my hips back in acceptance and was immediately rewarded with more dick.

The siren bred me roughly, pounding her full length in and out of my tight butt. I dug my fingers into the sand and rocked my hips back to every thrust. I was helpless to do more than moan; my voice was lost in a song of pleasure. My entire body felt so warm and tingly. Being fucked by the siren felt like falling into a bottomless pit of hugs.

My arms felt weak and gave out. My chest thudded against the sand. My knees remained strong and held my rump up for her. She leaned forward until I could feel her tits on my back and then kissed my neck. I came for her, spilling my load into the sand. She held that position, taking me even harder now.

I couldn't imagine anywhere I'd rather be. This beautiful creature was not only gracing me with her presence, but honoring me with her body as well. The sound of her moans, so close to my ears, drove me to a wonderful sort of madness.

"Cum with me, my love!"

I wouldn't have been able to resist her even if I wanted to. She pushed herself deep inside and released a truly musical cry of ecstasy. My voice mingled with hers, and we made perfect harmony. Another load of my seed splattered uselessly onto the sand, while hers filled my backside with glorious warmth.

Life with the siren was more wonderful than anything I could have ever imagined. The cave was empty, that was where I slept each night. It was damp and almost perpetually cold, but in a good way. It was where she allowed me to stay when she didn't need me. She brought me fish from the sea and fresh fruit from trees near town. I was fed only as much as I needed to avoid starvation, but that made it easy to stay in shape. She wouldn't let me leave the cove, so it was hard to exercise, but I never had to worry about getting lost! Or stolen, which would be oh so much worse.

To my surprise, I soon found that my seed had fertilized the siren's eggs. She laid a clutch one day and charged me with protecting them in her absence. I did so gladly; I wouldn't ever allow anything to happen to my beautiful children. In time, the eggs hatched, freeing siren chicks in a variety of colors. They were all feminine, like their mother. Or, more accurately, they were all probably hermaphrodites. Like their mother.

Our first brood consisted of only three chicks. Their human flesh was pale like their mother's, but their feathers were in different colors; one black, one blue, and one yellow. I raised them with my mate, doing everything she advised to be the best father possible. Once our young were mature enough to fly, they left to find their own territories. Then, it was time to make more.

My life alternated between the mind-blowing pleasure of near-constant sex and the soul-felt joy of fatherhood. I realized that there never was a material treasure to be found here. The siren's song was the treasure, and it was the only treasure I'd ever need. That old man who sold me the map was wrong to fight her. He was a fool to pass up such a wonderful life.

15 VISITOR

I had always been fascinated by tentacles. Even when I was young, the octopus was my favorite animal. As an adult, my interest expanded to include hentai. My friends think I'm strange, but I don't care. Something about the way tentacles move just fascinates me, beyond all reason. I even bought a dildo shaped like the end of a tentacle, from an online toy store. But, one night, my wildest fantasies came true.

The evening began like almost any other. I had just come home from work and I was relaxing with a movie. By "movie," I mean tentacle hentai, and by "relaxing," I mean I was playing with myself. I'd been so eager to get started that I hadn't even fully undressed. I lay there, sprawled out on the couch, wearing just a T-shirt and socks, vigorously pumping my silicone tentacle in and out of my juicy pussy.

The animated women, on-screen, resisted the tentacles. It was so hard to find consensual tentacle hentai, but I could never imagine saying, "no," to a tentacle monster. The cartoon sex sped up, and soon, the beast creamed all three of the girls he was molesting. I rammed my toy tentacle deep into my own body and imagined it cumming in me. That was just what I needed to finish. I bucked my hips and cried out in ecstasy, squirting all over myself.

After I came down, from my peak, I writhed on the couch and half-listened to the anime characters exchange terrible dialogue. There was enough "plot" between sex scenes that I would be ready to go, again, by the time the next one started. Something to do with demons and world domination, it was kind of hard to follow.

Suddenly, I heard a loud crash from outside. I hopped up and went to investigate. Just as I reached the back door, I realized I was still naked from the waist down. I made a quick trip back to the living room to grab my shorts and headed outside.

Armed with only a flashlight, I stalked around the backyard. Nothing looked immediately out of place. I followed where I thought the sound had come from and, finally, spotted a potential source. There was a pond nearby. It was partially on my property. Great clouds of steam rolled off of the water's surface; the pond was practically boiling.

I shined my flashlight into the water, searching for a heat source. Near the edge, partially buried in the mud, was a meteorite. The space rock was still hot enough to glow, heated to a brilliant red-orange by atmospheric friction. It was pockmarked with holes of varying sizes, and looked as though it might be hollow.

I stared at the rock for a long while, watching it change colors as it cooled. I thought it might be worth something. I intended to pick it up, once it had cooled enough to touch. While I was staring, though, several green tentacles emerged from the holes in the rock and felt around.

At first, I thought, "I must be imagining things. Surely, I was watching too much hentai. Space tentacles can't be real." When those green tendrils touched me, though, I knew they were no hallucinations. The creature wrapped its tentacles around my breasts, squeezing them through my top. I moaned, especially, when those lovely tendrils found my stiff nipples, another tentacle ground against the crotch of my shorts, rubbing the fabric against my moist slit.

This was all getting me very hot very, quickly. I had always dreamed of having tentacle sex for real, but I never thought it would happen. I hesitantly stepped away from the tentacled molester and peeled out of my clothes. I didn't care if the neighbors saw me naked. With any luck, they were about to get more of a show than that.

I stepped forward, again, and the tentacles immediately began caressing my naked body. The slick, slimy warmth on my sensitive flesh sent tingles up and down my spine. More tentacles emerged from the water, their tips caressed and tickled along my entire body. They paid special attention to my nipples and slit, teasing me, exquisitely.

Suddenly, four tentacles gripped me tight, one on each arm and one on each leg. They lifted me into the air, holding my limbs spread. Two more tentacles coiled together, mashing their tips against each other. The double-tentacle buried itself firmly in my pussy, earning a surprised gasp and an excited buck. I squeezed around their combined girth, the real thing felt so much better than my toy.

The tentacles probed deep, all the way to my cervix. One stopped there, but the other kept going. The narrow tip nudged my cervix open and wriggled up, inside. I winced and clenched tight, but it kept going. It explored my uterus. I could feel the slimy tip poking around the walls of my womb.

Once satisfied with its exploration, the tentacle pulled out of my innermost sanctuary. It retreated, until it was even with its twin, then the coiled tentacles began to enthusiastically fuck me. They were going deeper than I liked, but I didn't care. I bucked my hips and cried out, passionately, every time those hot, slimy, green tendrils rammed up, inside me.

Another tentacle found its way into my open mouth and down my throat. I had practiced deep-throating my toy tentacle before, so my gag reflex was quite tamed. I happily sucked the tentacle using my lips and tongue to pleasure it as well as I knew how. I rather liked the sweet-sour flavor of the slime that coated my tentacled friend.

While I was distracted by the tentacles in my mouth and muff, another snuck around and tickled between my butt cheeks. I pressed back to it, eager for more. It accepted my nonverbal invitation and buried itself in my ass, with a single, hard push. I screamed around the tentacle in my mouth when I felt it going well past the natural stopping point. These tentacles were very flexible, and not limited to the straight stretch of my rectum. It slithered deeper and deeper, easily able to follow the twists and turns of my insides.

The tentacle in my mouth kept going deeper, as well, though at a significantly slower speed. The tentacles met inside my stomach, touched their tips together, then, both began pulling back. Once they'd both returned to more reasonable depths, they began to thrust in and out of me, just like the tentacles in my vagina.

I writhed in their grasp, blown away by the bounty of pleasure. Soon, a third tentacle buried itself in my quivering quim and coiled together, with its friends. Another tentacle found its way into my butt, as well. My lonely breasts were not left neglected for long; a pair of tentacles rose up to grasp them.

Tentacles coiled around my boobs and squeezed them, until I screamed. Then, they let up. They gently clenched and unclenched, massaging my tits. The tips stroked my nipples, coating them with hot slime in the process. While the tentacles were holding my boobs securely in place, another rose up to slide between them. It slithered forward, until it tapped my chin, then backed up. Then, it slid forward, again. I couldn't believe it; I was being tentacle tit-fucked!

The tentacles gradually sped up their respective motions. Soon enough, I was getting pounded hard. I screamed around the mouthful of slimy appendage and came around the trio of pussy-probing tentacles. To my surprise, they actually slowed down and helped me ride out my orgasm.

I wasn't given too much of a break, though, and the tentacles soon resumed the rough pounding. I wondered, briefly, if I had actually died and gone to some sort of wonderful, tentacled heaven. The thrusting grew more and more intense, swiftly driving me to the edge, once more.

I came, again, but the tentacles didn't slow down for me this time. They kept tearing me up, hard and fast. The overstimulation made me squirm in the air, but they held me tightly in place. I clenched my fists tight, digging my nails into my palms. My entire body shook and squirmed, beyond my ability to control it.

Just seconds after my orgasm, they had theirs. One of the tentacles in my pussy wedged itself up, into my womb; the other two pressed tight against my stretched cervix. Jets of thick, hot cum erupted into all three of my holes. The tentacles holding my arms, legs, and breasts ejaculated, as well. Their bright green goo splashed all over my body. The tentacle fucking my tits curled and shot its load all over my face; it got quite a bit in my hair, as well.

The tentacles gently laid me down in the grass. It stroked my sensitive body, rubbing their warm green spunk into my skin. The tentacle in my mouth had given me quite a load. I held some on my tongue, savoring it, like sweet liquid candy, before I swallowed. It was very thick. I could feel it slither down my throat, almost as though it were alive itself.

My alien friend wasn't done, though. When I opened my eyes, again, I saw all of the tentacles coiling together, into one super-tentacle. Before I could even wonder what it planned to do with that thing, the incredible thickness shoved itself into my pussy. I arched and screamed, spread unimaginably wide, by the combined girth of 13 tentacles. Their slime made an effective lubricant, allowing them to probe into my pussy, despite the ridiculous width.

I grasped at the monstrous bulk, feeling it slide between my hands, while it took me in smooth strokes. I cried out, in pain, every time it pushed its way into me, I could feel my insides rearranging to accommodate it. The sensation was amazing enough to be worth the discomfort, though. Every time the tentacles shoved themselves into my sloppy snatch, I got a little closer to another orgasm.

My legs began to shake, uncontrollably. It hit me all too soon. I let out a climactic wail and squirted on my lover's tentacles. Before I'd even fully finished, the mass of tendrils inside me began to spin. The tentacles untwisted inside me, then, twisted together in the opposite direction. That, alone, was enough to make me cum, yet again.

The tentacles gave me a few seconds to catch my breath, then, started pounding my stretched beaver, all over again. They took me hard and fast, making me cry out with every deep thrust. My oversensitive body couldn't handle it. In just a couple of minutes, I came again. This time, they joined me. All 13 tentacles ejaculated, at the same time. My belly swelled, a little, from the excessive cum load. Then, slime began flooding out, around the tentacles. They pulled out before they were done ejaculating and shot the rest of their combined load down the front of my body in broad stripes. I felt like I was being painted.

For a long while, I couldn't move. I just stayed there, on my back, in the grass, panting. Sticky, green slime covered my body, and it was beginning to get cold. I could feel it growing thicker, with the temperature drop. I was going to need a long shower and, perhaps, a squeegee.

After catching my breath, I sat up and saw a tentacled slime blob, sitting near me. The alien was translucent and green, with a glowing, white core at the center of its body. It was poking at my clothes with a couple of tentacles, exploring my bra. I pet him, while

I rested a bit more, only now, noticing that his surface felt remarkably like gelatin.

When I was finally able to stand, I gathered my clothes and picked up the alien. I cradled him between my breasts and walked back to the house. I didn't know, or care, what anyone else might do to him; he was coming home with me. He'd expressed his interest in humans clearly enough, and I was more than happy to cater to his needs.

16 WITCH'S BALL

The last day of summer was met with celebration in Watervale. A large, roughly rectangular clearing in the woods some distance from town served as the setting for a big party to bid the warm weather farewell and welcome the fall. That celebration was over a month ago, though. The field had been repurposed for a different kind of party. People in fancy clothes danced under the moonlight. An orchestra's worth of glowing instruments played themselves, providing the event with music.

However, none of the people were really human. At least, that's what the witch had told me. She transformed me without even asking and then brought me to the party and told me to mingle. The witch told me that everyone else here was transmogrified from something inhuman, but I didn't believe her. These people were having too much fun. They were too comfortable. I refused to believe that they were all really cats and dogs and broomsticks dancing in human form. As awkward as I felt on two legs, I imagined they would have to feel something approaching the same.

I envied them not only for their comfort in biped configuration, but for their comfort in clothes. The formal attire given to me by the witch felt so stiff and stuffy. I'd never worn clothes before, and it felt so constricting.

I felt clumsy; my every move was awkward and annoying. The others had to be true humans; there was no way they couldn't be. I was far too self-conscious to join in the revelry. They'd see how awkward I was, and then they'd know I was not one of them.

A voice startled me from behind. "You've been playing wallflower all night. Go mingle!"

I whirled around to face the witch. She had shed a good portion of her gown. The outfit that remained managed to be simultaneously fancy and revealing. A soft, silver-blue luminescence surrounded her. I couldn't tell if it was a sign of her power, or if it was the moonlight reflecting off of her exposed skin. The display of cleavage and thigh made me feel strange, no doubt a side-effect of my temporarily human body.

"What do you expect me to do here? I don't know the first thing about being human!"

"Neither did anyone else here. Haven't you ever wanted to see what it's like, though?"

"Honestly? No. I had a good life before."

The witch laughed. "Go socialize! Eat, drink, dance! Do anything you like, just stop moping! You can go back to being a skittish loner when you're in your own body."

"What if they know I'm not really human?"

"I told them the same thing I told you. They were all transformed, just like you. Nobody here was born human."

"Not even you?"

The witch laughed again. "I'm really a dragon, dear. I just find the human body to be more convenient."

"I don't believe you. These people move too easily. They're too comfortable in human form to be anything else."

"Do you know what separates you from them? They aren't embarrassed. They don't care about what the others think of them. They want to have fun before midnight. They're enjoying their human bodies, while you stand around worrying about how silly you'll look if you do the same."

"This body is so ridiculous and clumsy!"

"Your movements don't look as awkward as they feel, I assure you. That body knows how to move itself just fine, even if the motions feel awkward to your brain."

"I just don't know..."

"Well sweetie, you'll be yourself again at the stroke of twelve. You've got about an hour left if you want to have some fun. If dancing doesn't interest you, have you considered trying sex as a human?"

I went wide-eyed and blushed. "With you?"

The witch grinned. "No, not unless you really want to. Just quit being so shy and talk to someone. Find yourself a nice young woman, or maybe a nice young man. See what it's like to mate in a body like this."

"I don't know who to talk to. Everyone else is having so much more fun than I am."

"Not that girl." The witch grabbed my shoulders and spun me around to face a chubby lady, sitting alone on a bench. "She's been sitting there alone all night. Poor girl looks like she could use a friend. Why don't you join her? Talk to her, dance with her, see how the night goes."

"What if she doesn't like me?"

"It can't hurt to try. After midnight you won't have the chance. Now shoo, shoo! Stop moping around!"

The witch gently pushed me in the plump woman's direction. Reluctantly, I started walking. I avoided the other guests on the way. This woman did look like she could use some company, and I didn't want to get distracted by anybody else.

She wore a sequined black dress that made her sparkle in the moonlight. Despite the eye-catching clothes, nobody seemed to be paying attention to her. Her hair was bright orange, tied back in a ponytail. She simply sat on the bench, alone, contemplating the grass.

I fought the butterflies in my stomach and mustered the courage to speak. "Anyone sitting here?"

The lady jerked, apparently startled by my voice. "Um, no. You can sit there if you want. I don't mind."

I sat next to her and offered a smile. My eyes explored her nicely rounded figure while she eyed my lithe frame. "You look like you could use some company."

"I'm all right. I just don't know what I'm supposed to do here. These people all seem so much more human than me."

"I know, I feel the same way! The witch just told me that we feel more awkward than we look, though. Something to think about."

"Is that so? Hmm..." She glanced away, thinking about something. "How long have you known the witch?"

"Pretty much just tonight. I live near her, but I don't even know her name."

"Same here. I think she just transformed a bunch of random animals and objects into people."

"That's what she told me. Everyone except that guy with the black hair, there." I pointed at the man. "He was her cat, I think. The way he hovers around her like that gives him away—he does the same in cat form."

"So you live close enough to observe how her cat behaves?"

"In my real body, not understanding how a cat behaves would mean certain death."

The woman giggled. "I thought you

seemed kind of mousy."

"That obvious, huh? Yes, I was a mouse before tonight. I live in the witch's walls. What were you?"

My new friend blushed. "I don't want to talk about it. Leave it to say human form is a huge change for me." There was a brief, awkward silence before she resumed speaking. "So, what's your name?"

"It's, uh..." I glanced down at the name embroidered on the cuff of my jacket, positioned for convenient reference. The witch had thought ahead and assigned us all human names. "Doug? I'm Doug, apparently."

"I'm Carol. Nice to meet you, Doug."

"Likewise, Carol. Would you like to dance with me?"

"Oh, I don't know how to dance."

"Neither do I. Let's go look silly together."

"Are you suggesting we become a couple, Doug?"

"If you'd have me. We only have an hour, let's make it mean something."

"Goodness, is it that late already? The concept of time is new to me. I was going to just sit here until I revert. But there's something about you, Doug. Something that I like. I think I would like to dance with you."

We stood up together and made our way to the middle of the field. The two of us attempted to move to the rhythm of the music. Carol looked like she was doing all right, but I felt incredibly goofy. I tried to believe what the witch said about looking less awkward than I felt, but it did little good. Despite how clumsy I felt, Carol didn't seem to mind my dancing.

The music changed after a little while. The band of magically animated instruments now played a much slower tempo. Carol danced closer to me, pressing her body against mine. I could feel her body heat. The closeness gave me some odd, unexpected feelings. I leaned in and kissed her softly on the lips. The contact made my flesh tingle.

Carol blushed, and then moved close to whisper in my ear. "Let's go somewhere a little more private and get you out of those clothes."

"Are you sure?"

"We have less than an hour to be together. I want you inside me while there's still time."

I could see the passion burning in Carol's eyes. Her lust was contagious, and made my pants feel tighter. I took her hand and led her away from the party. Just before we entered tree cover, I spotted the witch out of the corner of my eye. I glanced her way. She smiled and winked at me.

Carol and I walked through the woods together. We didn't stop until we could just barely hear the music. In a small clearing, we kissed again. Our hands roamed over each other's bodies, unfastening buttons and tugging at laces. The cloth loosened around both of us. When our lips parted, we hurriedly pulled off our own garments and threw them to the ground.

The sight of Carol's nude body thrilled me, I assume because of my temporarily human sensibilities. She had large, plump breasts. Her erect, pink nipples stood out in the cold air. Her belly had some appealing curvature. She wasn't obese by any means, nor was she at all thin. Somewhere in-between, which I found appealing. Her thighs were thick, and she had a big, round bottom.

When my eyes drifted back to her face, I noticed her looking down and smiling. I glanced at my own crotch and gasped. "Good god! Are all humans so large?" My semi-erect cock was larger than my entire body used to be, by quite a bit.

"I wouldn't know, I've never seen one of those before! I like that it's big, it looks like fun! It's all droopy and sad, though. Let me cheer it up for you."

Before I could say a word, Carol was on her knees. She kissed the tip of my half-mast penis, then wrapped her lips around the head and suckled. Her tongue slid into my foreskin and teased the sensitive glans within. Pleasant tingles ran through me, and I could feel my member growing stiff in her mouth. She teased it to full hardness, and then took it further into her maw.

I watched, dumbfounded, as Carol bobbed her head on my length. One of her hands cupped my balls; I could see the other moving around between her own legs. There was no way she hadn't done this before, it felt too good to be her first time. Or perhaps it was something else the witch had anticipated.

To my surprise and disappointment, she stopped. That wonderful mouth slipped off of my rock hard dick. It was fully erect now, and covered in a thin layer of saliva. I was blown away by its size; it looked ridiculously large on my slender figure. Carol seemed quite pleased with my endowment, though.

"How do you want me?"

"What do you mean?"

"Which position? I can't wait anymore. I need you."

"How about all fours? That one seems...natural."

Carol turned away from me and put her hands on the ground. She waved her big, squeezable ass at me. I wasted no time in mounting her. The instant my thick tip pierced her mound, I lost control. My hips rolled on autopilot, bucking of their own accord. I drove my full length into her again and again at lightning speed, unable to slow or stop myself. My hips audibly slapped her ass with each slam, sending ripples throughout her round body.

Her moans were like music to my ears. Though the swift humping had at first alarmed me, my worries dissolved. She was definitely enjoying this. I clutched her love handles while savagely dicking her wet snatch. She was very lubricous, and took my girth easily.

Carol's body was very hot and tight inside. The feeling was incredible. I had never mated in my real body, and couldn't help but wonder if it would feel the same. Entirely on impulse, I released one of Carol's sides and slapped her fat ass.

My lover yelped, then wiggled. "Again!"

I grinned and smacked her bottom a second time. "You like that?"

"Oh, yes! Spank me!"

I got my other hand involved as well. I slapped one cheek, then the other. After a few alternating swats, I spanked both cheeks simultaneously. Then, I squeezed her ass tightly. I could see my fingers dig into her soft tush. The sight turned me on.

Carol's orgasm took me by surprise. Her back arched, her voice rose into a scream, and her pussy squeezed me like a vice. I hadn't realized how close I was, either. The added tightness finished me off almost immediately. I buried my shaft in her snatch and cried out. My pole pulsed within her, spurting thick gobs of my seed into her depths.

I leaned forward and wrapped my arms around Carol. I stayed that way for a few minutes, fully within her. I savored her warmth, her tightness, and the closeness that we shared. She stroked my arm while I held her.

"That was wonderful, Doug. Can we do it again?"

"I would love to."

"I want to try it face to face this time."

"All right."

I pulled out of Carol's pussy. My twitching manhood was still fully erect. The mixture of fluids made it glisten in the moonlight. A soft breeze picked up, giving me chills.

Carol rolled onto her back in the grass, looking up at me expectantly. I knew there wasn't much time left, and didn't hesitate to mount my lover. I wrapped my arms around her and slid deep into her loins. We moaned in unison, and my body rutted her of its own accord.

Her body moved as well, bucking her hips up in perfect rhythm to meet each of my thrusts. It felt even better than last time. Our bodies slapped together noisily while our moans coalesced into a song of passion.

Carol's lips pressed forcibly against mine. Our tongues wrestled while our groins butted together. I could feel her nails raking down my back. After a minute or so, I broke the kiss and moved my attention lower. I kissed her neck, and then licked her cleavage. My lips and tongue teasingly explored one of her impressive breasts. The instant my lips came in contact with her stiff nipple, I stopped teasing and sucked her tit.

My lover's moans grew in volume, and encouraged me to keep doing what I was doing. I swirled my tongue around her areola in broad circles. Then, I flicked my tongue swiftly back and forth across the nip.

I felt Carol's hands move further down my back, until she was touching my rump. My bottom was flat and bony, but she did her best to squeeze it, anyway. I could feel something welling up inside, and knew I was getting ready to blow again.

"Cum with me, Doug!"

I nodded my approval without breaking lip lock with her nipple. In just a few more passion drenched seconds, we threw our heads back in unison. We moaned together, a single sound of mutual ecstasy. She clenched tight around me, and my rocket burst into her once more. This climax was so breathtakingly intense that I didn't notice Carol had gone silent below me.

Once I regained my senses and opened my eyes, I noticed that the world around me had gotten much bigger. I had reverted to my natural form, I could feel it. Four legs, fur, a naked tail, whiskers, round ears. I had become a mouse mid-orgasm. My softening cock was pressed against a crease in a hard surface.

I was a little afraid to find out what had become of Carol. The thought of being physically incompatible with her now scared me. Hesitantly, I looked down. I stood upon a large, lustrous, orange object. Carol was, in fact, a pumpkin. My softening mouse dick rested in one of her crevices, where I'd cum on her. I sat up on my hind legs and curled my body to clean myself up, then licked the mouse spunk off of her orange surface.

I pressed my forelegs against her in a vain attempt at a hug. I didn't know if she could feel it, or even notice. I didn't want to leave her side, but I knew I had to get home. I was a house mouse; I knew nothing of surviving in the woods.

Eventually, I brought myself to climb off

of the pumpkin. It was a little disorienting to see the woods from so close to the ground, but I found my way back to the field. It was littered with books, brooms, gardening tools, silverware, fruit, and various other things. A few confused-looking animals hung around; dogs, cats, mice, bats, squirrels, and birds. I passed by all of them and made my way to the witch's house.

I returned to my living space within the walls. It was the life I was accustomed to, something comfortable in its familiarity. However, I would never forget the night I spent as a human. I couldn't get Carol out of my mind. I often wonder if she still thinks of me, or if pumpkins can even think at all.

AUTHOR'S NOTE

Readers: I want to expand a few of the stories to see where the characters can be explored further. If there are any of the stories that you would like to read more about again, I'd love to hear from you!

Visit my blog at www.blaineteller.com

Join my newsletter for free exclusive previews
http://www.blaineteller.com/in

Follow me on Twitter at
http://www.twitter.com/blaineteller

Like my page on Facebook at
http://www.facebook.com/blaineteller

Discover my books at major ebook retailers everywhere.